Bob Moats

I0567066

Santa Murders

By Bob Moats

Santa Murders

For information and address:
Magic 1 Productions
P.O. Box 524, Fraser MI 48026-0524
Website: http://murdernovels.com
Cover by Bob Moats
Stock photo from Fotosearch.com

Bob Moats

Other Jim Richards series books by Bob Moats

For a preview or to purchase a book, go to
http://murdernovels.com

What a few people are saying about Murder Novels by Bob Moats

Mr. Moats, I just got your novel "Classmate Murders" and have to let you know, I read it in one evening. That is the first book I have ever done that with. That was the most enjoyable book I have ever read. I just started reading e-books, and reading again, after getting my wife a Kindle. This book was my 12th, and the best. I just got Las Vegas Showgirls to (read) tomorrow evening. I look forward to reading many of your books in this series. I have been searching for an author and books that were fun, entertaining reads. Your books are just the ticket.

Regards, A new fan, Bill from South Carolina

****

Another very nice comment submitted through my website from Micki P.:

"I recently was given a kindle for my 60th birthday. The first book I downloaded was the Classmate Murders and have now read every one of the them. Today I started on the Fatal Rejection series. Thank you for the wonderful ride with Jim and Penny and all the rest of the troop. I have laughed and giggled thru the stories, my poor family gave me the strangest looks! Now I really want a little Yorkie!! Fatal Rejection so far is another great read! I will be looking out for more of Jim Richards and since you are my #1 Author, anything of yours I can find."

Extra special thanks to:

Special thanks to Val Brooks who edited this book and for her great suggestions.

Thank you to all the people who purchased this book. I hope you enjoy it as much as I enjoyed writing it for my faithful readers.

The Jim Richards Family of Readers is listed in the back of the book.

Santa Murders
by Bob Moats

Chapter 1

The man liberally applied the spirit gum glue to his chin and cheeks. He wanted to be sure the fake beard wouldn't come loose or fall off. He spread the sticky liquid to his upper lip and then pressed the hairs of the white beard and mustache to his skin. He patted carefully along the edges so the glue didn't ooze out through the hair. He sat back and admired the new look in the mirror of the dressing table. It pleased him. He stood and went to a chair where a "fat suit" hung and pulled it on. His belly was now like a "bowl full of jelly" and he gave a happy laugh that came out, "Ho, ho, ho," and filled the room with his deep voice. He pulled on the red velour pants trimmed nicely with white fur and tightened his belt. Then he pulled on the black boots and lastly, shrugged into a coat of the same velour material as the pants, fully covering his big fake belly.

He stood in front of the full length mirror hanging on the wall, took a cap from the hook next to it and pulled it on his head. He straightened out the bright white wig that was attached to the cap and was satisfied as he turned around in front of the mirror, checking out his outfit. Perfect, he thought, a nice disguise for what he was going to do. Very seasonal and something that no one would suspect him of committing crimes in.

He went to a table next to his bed and picked up the 9mm handgun and lifted his coat, placing the gun under the belt holding up his pants. He straightened the coat and took one last look in the mirror. Seeing no bulge indicating he was carrying a gun, he was now ready to commit murder.

~~*~~

Penny and I had gotten through the Thanksgiving festivities with all our friends at Angelo's restaurant. I had booked his big banquet room for everyone and had them prepare a special turkey meal with all the trimmings. Everyone in my firm of investigators, along with Deacon and Lynn, were there and having fun. My daughter Carol joined us after she personally made sure all our food was prepared properly. I insisted that Angelo and his lady friend Sophia join us, along with Fred, the newest addition to our family.

Santa Murders

Fred was settling in with us and I was glad he was out of the homeless life. He was taking care of the building, both cleaning and landscaping, and was our live-in night watchman. He and Buck had fixed up the room in Buck's old office in the store room, turning it into a small living space. I think Buck took a real liking to Fred.

The Thanksgiving feast was a memory now as Penny and I were navigating the Boulevard Mall on 'Black Friday' seeking out presents for Christmas. I wasn't fond of shopping with Penny, she would always make a big production out of it. But this was for Christmas and it was the one time of the year I didn't mind shopping with her. Of course, I'd have to go shopping by myself for gifts for Penny, and I had no idea what to buy her. I still had time since Christmas was a month away.

"Will you quit being so slow moving," Penny said as I was daydreaming about what to buy her.

"I'm sorry, but I was just thinking something," I replied.

"Well, stop thinking, it gets you in trouble."

I smiled and followed her to the company van with our packages in hand. I took the van because I knew Penny would fill it, and she did. We dumped our latest booty in and she turned to me and said,

"We need to go to a baby store to get presents for little PJ."

I pulled out my Samsung Note 3 phone and brought up Google. I searched for baby stores around Las Vegas and said, "Babies "R" Us over on Rainbow Boulevard would do the trick." She agreed, so we drove there and she led the attack. After an hour of Penny checking out all the baby things, she picked out a few toys and necessities for Lynn and Deacon's baby.

Back at the van, we dumped everything in and drove home. Our puppy Willy was going crazy when I opened the door, so I took him out for a run and a dump. Penny was unloading the van and taking everything into the house.

I was standing on the lawn watching Willy fertilize a small patch, when I saw a car driving up the road. It was Will Trapper. He was spending a lot of time with his girlfriend Sam, so I saw little of him around the office. That was fine with me, it wasn't like we all had to be at work. We were independent and could pick our crime investigations as we wanted. It didn't make Lacey happy, but she endured.

He pulled into the drive and Willy made a bee line to him as he got out.

"Hey, there's my namesake," he said as he picked up the tiny dog. "Jim, are you busy?"

Santa Murders

"Penny and I just got back from Christmas shopping, but I'm done now. What's up?"

"I got a call from an old friend of mine, old as in age. He asked if I could help him with a problem." He put Willy down and we walked to the porch to get out of the hot sun. Willy ran to the door waiting for us.

"Okay, what's the problem that I feel you want me to help with?"

"He's a Santa Claus for one of the local charitable organizations in the city and he has been getting death threats. Now, I can't imagine who'd want to murder Santa Claus, but he asked me to help him."

"The death threats started when?"

"As soon as he started to go out and ring his bell for money. He was getting notes in his pot, mixed in with the money, warning him to stop playing Santa or he'd regret it."

"Just saying he'd regret it, no actual death threat?" I asked.

"Well, not in so many words. But he's really worried. I can't imagine there's a Santa union that's muscling in on the Christmas bell-ringing Santas.

That would be a first for me. Or a mob wanting a cut of the money. I figure if we watch over the guy and see who is doing this, well, I thought in the spirit of Christmas, you'd want to help." He grinned and waited for me to respond.

"Ho, Ho, No," I replied, with a bigger grin. "After the Trick-or-Treat Killer, I'm done with holiday cases. Besides, Penny and I may go for a late Thanksgiving back home in Michigan. Just close family, and I know Penny would murder me if I got on a new case. See if Earl will help, he loves covert operations. He'd be happy to do surveillance on a Santa."

"You're getting to be a Scrooge in your old age," Trapper said with a laugh. "I thought I'd give you a shot at it first."

"Who's getting shot?" came a voice from the front door. It was Penny.

"Hi, Penny. I was just asking Jim if he'd like to protect the life of Santa Claus."

"Does Santa need protecting?" she said as she came out of the house and moved over to us.

"This one does. He's a friend of mine and he's been threatened. He asked me to help him."

Penny looked at me and said, "You'd let Santa get hurt? Why?"

"He's not really Santa, and Will can protect him. Besides, we had talked about going back to Michigan for a late Thanksgiving," I said.

"We can do that at Christmas, I'd prefer it. Now, you need to save Christmas like you saved Halloween."

"But I didn't save Halloween. I didn't even save the killer," I said.

Penny turned to Trapper and said, "He'll help you, or he'll get a lump of coal in his stocking."

They both looked at me, I was being ganged up on, so what could I say, "Merry Christmas."

*

Chapter 2

"Okay, I'll bite," I said. "Let's go in the house and you can give me the details."

The three of us and the dog went in and Penny went off to sort the presents. I knew I'd be up late wrapping gifts. Trapper and I went to the snack bar and sat.

"Now, who is this friend of yours?" I asked.

"His name is Harold Renford. I knew him back when I was on the Metro LVPD as a bike cop. He was a street preacher and would stand on different corners extolling the word of God before we would tell him to move along. He did have a church in a small store front building that he owned from an inheritance from his father. The father was Oscar Renford, a wealthy financier who helped pay for building a number of the casinos in Vegas. Unfortunately, Harold and Oscar didn't see eye to eye about things and Harold was left with a building and little else. Harold didn't care, he had his little church and his street corners where he let people know where his church was."

"Did his church draw in anyone?"

"Surprisingly, yes. They were mostly street people, the homeless kind, like Fred was. I often suspected Harold had money stashed away somewhere, he always had food and drink for his followers." Trapper smiled and said, "He was regarded as a savior himself."

"How did he become Santa?"

"He did this every year. He worked with a couple shelters and helped raise money to keep them going. He always seemed to bring in the most donations every year. I think he salted the pot using his own money."

"If he had money stashed away, why didn't he just give it to the shelters?"

"Harold probably could have, I don't know why not, but I don't really know if he had much money. He enjoyed dressing up as Santa and he survived all these years somehow. His followers certainly didn't put money in any plate in his church." Trapper paused and thought. "Actually, as I think about it, Harold never did pass a plate. So he must have had the funds to live on and keep his church going. I'm sure the taxes on the building alone are enough to break any building owner."

"Maybe someone knows he has money and is trying to scare him for it."

"That's possible. I can't think of any other reason for threatening him. I figure if we could watch Harold and see if anyone slips a note, then we can nab whoever it is."

"Sounds easy enough. When does he go out and ring his bell?" I asked.

"He starts his day early and he's usually out at the Boulevard Mall."

"I didn't see any bell-ringing Santas at the mall when Penny and I were there. I usually drop a few bills in the pot."

"I told him to wait until I talked to you before he goes back out in public. He was so shook up by the notes, he agreed."

"Okay, I need to meet Harold and we need to work on a plan for surveillance. Is he inside or outside the mall?" I asked.

"Usually he's right at the doors just before going in. The mall overlooks him out there. They just don't want a ton of Santas all over inside the mall."

"Yeah, don't want to traumatize children seeing too many Santas. Where is he now?"

"At his church. Want to take a ride over and talk?"

"I'll let Penny know we are leaving," I said and went into the spare bedroom where she had presents all over the place. "Having fun?"

"I love this time of year. Since I have no family of my own, I'm happy to share yours. Plus all our great friends."

"I'm going with Will to see his Santa friend. I'll be back later."

"Just be sure to come back and help me wrap," she said, as she continued sorting boxes.

"I will." I went back out to the living room and said, "Let's go, quickly."

~~*~~

Santa walked through the casino being called to by the tourists. He would smile and wave, then walk on towards his destination. He would occasionally pat his coat to make sure the gun was tucked safely in the belt. He reached in his huge right pocket and came out with small handbill flyers and handed them to various people as he went on. Most people looked at them hoping they were some gimmick for a complimentary free night stay at the hotel. They frowned when it turned out to be a religious handbill.

Santa moved up to the restaurant lounge towards the back of the casino overlooking the gambling festivities. He walked past the hostess as she asked him if he'd like a seat. She frowned when he ignored her, walking on to a table with three men in suits. Santa stopped at the table as one man asked, "Too early for a present, isn't it?"

"Not for this." Santa reached under his coat, pulled the handgun, and then fired point-blank at one man. "This is God's punishment, you heathen," he called loudly, and threw more of his handbills into the air. He retreated quickly towards the back of the restaurant, through the kitchen doors, and out the back door to the alley.

The panic in the restaurant was elevating to horror as the man at the table slumped to the floor. The hostess called for hotel security and explained that they needed Metro police. There had been a shooting.

By the time LVMPD arrived, the restaurant was cleared by hotel security. The first responders examined the situation and one patrol officer called for homicide. Deacon DeAngelo took the call.

Santa Murders

~~*~~

Trapper pulled into the small parking area next to the huge building on Industrial Road just below Sahara Avenue. When we were driving by, I could see it was an old looking structure and in the middle of one storefront there was a sign—"God's Little Acre"—hand painted on a four by eight sheet of plywood above the door.

"That's Harold's church," Trapper said.

"Interesting looking. Does Harold own the entire building or just the church?"

"He owns the whole block. All the buildings you see along here. His father screwed up when he left the property to Harold. He didn't specify how much Harold would get. So he owns everything here."

"He's got to have money to pay for all the taxes." I was looking around at all the continuing construction going on beyond Harold's property— new hotels and casinos. "Why doesn't he sell all this and go to the Bahamas?"

"Harold grew up here and has many friends. I don't think he'd be happy anywhere else. Shall we go talk?"

We got out of Trapper's Jeep, and went over to the church. The door was unlocked and we entered. There were a number of chairs facing a small stage, and to the right was a long row of tables with coffee urns and numerous coolers I presumed held either food, drinks or snacks.

I was checking out the building. It was a huge single room with high walls going up to a ceiling that was at least twenty feet above us. Overhead was a huge oval skylight and there was a railing going around a circular opening that must be a second level. The building looked old and hadn't been restored from whatever it was years back.

A young man saw us and came over. "May I help you gentlemen?"

"Yeah, we need to see Harold," Trapper said.

"I'm sorry, Harold had to run out on an errand. He was wearing his Santa suit so I presume he was visiting one of the shelters to spread his joy."

*

Chapter 3

"He said he wouldn't be long, if you want to wait. There's coffee in the urns or soda pop in the coolers," he said, and motioned to the tables.

"Thanks, we'll wait," Trapper said and went straight to the coffee. "Want a cup?"

"How long have you known me? I don't drink coffee," I said as I opened one of the coolers. I found a Pepsi in water that must have been ice at one time.

"I told him not to go out in public. I know he was always pig-headed, but he seemed genuinely worried about the threats."

"Maybe he figured the Santa suit would disguise him. There are a good number of Santas out there right now. Hard to tell if it's him."

"I'll give you that one. I just don't like him doing this. He asked me to protect him and I can't if he doesn't listen."

"Well, not much you can do now but wait." I went to one of the chairs and sat. Trapper joined me, sipping his coffee.

"Harold never could make decent coffee," he said with a scowl.

We had been waiting about thirty minutes when the front door opened and in came Deacon with four officers holding on to their weapons. Deacon looked shocked when he saw us.

"What are you doing here?" he asked, coming over to us.

"Waiting. What are you doing here, and with back-up?" I asked.

He looked around and signaled to his men to spread out.

"What's going on?" Trapper asked Deacon.

"We're looking for Harold Renford, on suspicion of murder. Is he here?"

"Murder?" Trapper said as he stood. "You must be wrong, Harold would never murder anyone."

Deacon pulled out a couple handbills and handed them to Trapper. "Do these look familiar?"

Trapper read one and said, "Yes, they're from here. Harold's church. Where did you get them?"

"There was a Santa who entered the Venetian Hotel casino and went to the lounge in the back of the casino, shot a man, threw his flyers in the air and left. He did say, 'This is God's punishment, you heathen' according to witnesses, and then he fled the scene. We identified the flyers and came here. Is he here or not?"

"No, we were waiting for him. Who was murdered?"

"Mickey Collisi," he replied.

"Mickey Collisi, the mobster?" Trapper said, surprised. "If Harold did murder him, and I'm not saying he did, he should get a medal."

"I can't say out loud that I agree, but I do. Now why would Renford kill Collisi?"

"Harold wasn't involved with the mob. Not that I knew. I can't imagine why he'd want to kill one of their top bosses. Harold should be worried about the mob wanting his hide now."

"Yea, well, I got to take him in. Do you know where he is?"

"Nope, the kid said he thinks Harold went to run errands." Trapper didn't say anything about Harold wearing the suit. I hoped he did it deliberately.

The officers came back and said Renford wasn't in the building.

"Okay, sit and wait," he told them. They gathered and went to sit in the chairs on the other side of us.

"Deacon, I know Harold, he's not the kind to murder anyone. Let alone a mob boss."

"I don't know the man, I just know he's the prime suspect in this murder. Santa with these flyers, it points to your friend."

"Anyone can wear a Santa suit and shoot someone, then pass out incriminating handbills. Why would Harold murder, then pass out evidence to point to him?"

Deacon was silent for a moment, then said, "It doesn't make sense, I agree, but we have to take him in to find out what's going on. He's our number one suspect."

We sat quietly as Deacon paced the room looking at the posters on the walls. Trapper nodded to me and looked out the front window. I followed his nod and saw a car across the street. In the car was a Santa Claus watching the building and all the cop cars out front. I looked back to Trapper as he stood.

"You don't need us here, you can wait for him. I got better things to do," Trapper said.

"Yeah, I got Christmas presents to wrap with Penny. So I think we aren't needed here."

Deacon gave us a suspicious eye, but smiled. "Thanks guys, I'll let you know what happens."

We left through the front door and Trapper covertly signaled to the man in the car to go right, where his car was parked. We casually moved there and then around the building. Luckily the car was parked around the side and could not be seen by Deacon in the church. The car with Santa drove up and he rolled down the window. The man still had his beard and mustache on, but the cap and wig were gone.

"Will, what's going on? I saw all the police cars and didn't know whether to go in or not," Santa said.

"Harold, you know where I live, go there, we'll meet you. Now move quickly before the cops see you."

Bob Moats

The man spun out onto Industrial, turning down south. My office was on Industrial and Trapper said we'd go there and get my car. We drove down and arrived at the parking lot in back. I got out and went to my car.

"I'll see you at your place," I yelled to him as I got in my car.

We drove to Trapper's apartment and I parked. I saw Santa's car across the lot by Trapper's building, the two men standing next to it talking. I walked over to join them.

"Why am I here and what do the cops want?" Santa was saying to Trapper as I approached.

"Okay, let's go inside and work this out," Trapper said and led us to his apartment.

We were inside and Trapper locked the door. Santa had pulled off the beard and mustache and looked like a normal person.

"Harold, sit," Trapper commanded. Harold sat. "Okay, this is Jim Richards. He owns the investigating firm I'm part of and he's a good person. So talk to me. Where were you today?"

Harold paused a bit too long, looking like he wanted to talk but didn't.

"Harold, the cops were there to arrest you on suspicion of murder."

Harold's face went as white as the fake beard he held. "Murder! Who?"

"Mickey Collisi. Do you know him?" Trapper asked.

"No, never heard of him. Who is he?"

"He's a big mob boss from out East, and they say a Santa went into a restaurant and shot him dead. Then the killer passed out your flyers. You don't know anything about this?"

"Will, I don't know anything about this."

"Okay, we need to establish an alibi for you. Where were you this afternoon?"

"I can't say," was all he said.

"Harold, you don't understand. It looks good that you did this. It's all circumstantial right now, but they can make your life miserable. Where were you?"

"I can't say. Really, I can't. It's personal and I'm not able to tell you."

"Harold, you asked me to protect you. I can't if you don't cooperate. If you tell me, I'll keep your secret safe. I've already committed a crime by harboring you away from the cops. I need to know where you were."

Harold sat quietly for a while. We waited. Then he said, "I was with a woman."

*

Chapter 4

Trapper's mouth dropped and then shut. "A woman, Harold? I've never known you to be with a woman. Why now, and who?"

"I can't tell you who. She's married to someone important in the city. It wouldn't be good for her to be exposed."

"Oh, great. Your air-tight alibi, that would take suspicion away from you, is someone you can't reveal to us. Harold, you're looking at murder charges if they find you. How important is this woman to risk your life?"

He sat there looking miserable, not speaking. Then he said quietly, "She's married to a big hotel owner and if she were exposed, she would lose everything. They have a pre-nup that states she gets nothing for infidelity."

"So, her being rich outweighs your life. Harold, Nevada still has the death penalty. I've had a good number of lovers, married or otherwise, but my life is more important than a fling."

"It's not a fling," Harold said bristling. "She's something to me. I feel great when I'm with her."

Trapper turned to me. "Jim, how many romances end up with the married person divorcing their spouse and going off with their lover? Extremely few, if any," Trapper said, not waiting for my answer. "One reason why a lot of women and men fool around with married people, they know they won't get stuck with someone who was unfaithful to their spouse."

Trapper turned back to Harold and moved closer, bending down. "Listen to me old friend. I don't want you to get hurt, but this romance won't go anywhere, you will go to prison, maybe even death row. I don't want to see that."

He waited for Harold to say something. "Harold, how important is this woman to you?"

Harold had his head down and said quietly, "Very."

Trapper stood up and sighed. "Well, when she decides money is more important than you, she's gone." He turned back to me. "Okay, change of plan, we need to find this rogue Santa fast, to clear Harold. The cops and the mob will be looking for him. I think he needs to stay here for his own good."

"Will, you're harboring a fugitive. I don't want to see you go down too. Let's get him one of those motel rooms uptown, and I'm sure he won't say you were involved if they find him."

"I think we need to get him out of town for his own good. The mob has long fingers, and the cops won't have too much trouble finding one man dressed as Santa."

"Unfortunately, they're looking only for Santa Harold," I said. "They won't be looking for anyone else."

"Which is why we need to find the bastard. Let's get Harold into a safe place, then we can investigate." Trapper turned back to Harold. "Listen, we're going to get you out of town and into hiding, for your own good. Forget your flame, if she loves you, she can wait until we solve this. Now, get out of that Santa outfit. I may have some clothes that will fit you." He turned back to me, "Jim, I know someone over in Boulder City who can watch Harold. He's kind of a former criminal who owes me a big favor."

"Let's do it. We're both in trouble now, so let's get it done."

We spent a short time getting Harold changed and then Trapper called his friend explaining what we needed. He smiled when he hung up and said, "Gus said he will help. We have to move quickly before Deacon finds out Harold is a friend of mine. I know Deacon well enough, he may seem dumb, but he's pretty quick putting two and two together." He went to the window and looked out. "The police shouldn't know what Harold looks like, unless they pulled up his driver's license. It looks clear outside, let's go."

We exited the apartment, but I stopped at the parking lot. "Will, what about Harold's car? If the cops find it here, they'll know he's with you."

Trapper asked Harold for his keys and threw them to me. "Follow me, then we'll dump the car in a parking lot somewhere south. Make sure you wipe your prints off the wheel."

I caught the keys when Trapper threw them and went to the car, being careful with what I handled.

Trapper and Harold got into Trapper's Jeep and he drove out quickly, but not so fast to attract the attention of a roving patrol car. We stopped in a shopping mall parking lot and I parked Harold's car in a spot that wouldn't draw attention. I wiped down my prints, got into the Jeep, and we went off.

Trapper drove over to the 515 Highway and south to Boulder City. Harold was in the back seat, being quiet.

"Harold, how did you meet this mystery woman?" Trapper asked.

Harold cleared his throat and said, "About two weeks ago, I was playing Santa at a charitable party for the Good Will for All Soup Kitchen. She is on the board of directors, and she talked to me when I was taking a break. We got along well and she asked if I could see her privately."

"So she initiated the tryst. When did she tell you she couldn't leave her husband and why?"

"On our second meeting. I knew she was married, so I played it cool. Then she told me who her husband was. I wasn't happy about it, he could cause real trouble for me. About as bad as the mob. I met with her today to say I couldn't see her again. She wasn't happy, but what could she do? She didn't want to jeopardize her standing in the community."

Trapper didn't say anything more as we drove. I didn't know what to say, so I just enjoyed the ride.

Santa Murders

About forty minutes later, we arrived at the border of Boulder City. Trapper had been to his friend's house before so he knew the way. We pulled up a fairly deserted dirt road and to what looked like a farm house, complete with barn.

Trapper pulled into the drive and stopped. A rather tall, tanned, well-built man came out of the house and over to us.

We exited the car and Trapper went to the tall man. "Gus, thanks for doing this."

"No problem, Will," he replied with a gravelly voice, reminding me of a mobster.

"Gus, this is my friend Jim, and this man is Harold Renford, our fugitive."

"Pleased to meet y'all." He now had a twang of country in his voice. "Please come on in the house where we can talk."

We entered the house that was sparsely furnished and subtle. No trappings of technology, no computer, or even a TV. I wondered how a man could live like this for very long. I'd go nuts without my computers and television.

"Sit please," the man said. We did and he asked, "Would y'all like something to drink?"

"No thanks Gus, we need to get back to Vegas. To make this quick, I'll explain the situation." Trapper gave Gus the rundown on what had transpired today and finished.

"That's quite a story, Will. Sounds like something outta some crime novel. Good plot so far, you're goin' after the perp?"

I wondered if he read a lot of books. I looked over to another room and saw them. Tons of books on wall-sized shelves.

Trapper grinned and said, "Jim, Gus is a writer like you. Mostly crime fiction, not like that real stuff you write." He looked to Gus and said, "Jim is Jim Richards, he writes true crime books about our adventures in solving crimes."

Gus got a big smile, stood and went to a desk. He picked up a book and came to me.

"Mind autographing your latest book for me, Mr. Richards?"

*

Chapter 5

I was surprised, to say the least. I took the book and opened it to the title page and signed my name with my pen. "Please call me Jim, I'm not formal with friends. Do you publish your books?"

"I have a couple books on Amazon, nothing big, just self-published."

"I was in the process of doing that when I got picked up by a publisher. But, we aren't here for that. We need to help Harold." I handed the book back to him. He placed it on his desk again.

Gus turned back to Trapper, "Yes, I can take care of him. I'm sure you want me to keep him here and safe?"

Trapper stood. "Yep, don't let him get away from you. The police, and most likely the mob, are after him."

"Police, I avoid. The mob, I don't worry about." He had a strange smile and then I stood.

"Okay Harold, you have a safe place to hide out until Jim and I can find the real killer. Don't screw up by leaving."

Gus laughed, "He'd have a long walk since I don't have a car."

"Good, now you two get along. I'll call when we have any word on our findings."

Trapper reached in his pocket and took out a wad of cash, peeling a couple hundred dollar bills off, giving them to Gus for Harold's food and clothes, he said.

Trapper and Gus said their goodbyes and Gus told me he enjoyed my books. I told him I'd look up his books and read them. We went back out to the car and drove out the drive. Harold was standing on the porch looking distressed.

"I hope he doesn't give Gus too much trouble," I said.

"Gus can handle Harold. He used to be a mob lieutenant himself."

I about dropped my jaw when he said that. "Gus is a mob figure?"

"Was. Most of his people were killed off years ago and his small family broke up. He retired out here, and the Feds even stopped bothering him. He lives quietly now, but don't mess with him, he can be dangerous."

I turned to look back and Harold was gone from the porch. I hoped they'd get along.

We arrived back at the office and went in to find Deacon in the lobby talking to Lynn.

Deacon said, "Where have you two been off to?"

Trapper smiled, "We were out enjoying the beautiful fall weather."

"I hope that was all you were enjoying. I found out something."

"What? That you're a so-so detective," Trapper said with a grin.

"No, I found out you're a friend of Harold Renford. I don't suppose you've seen him lately?"

"Us, no we haven't. Have we Jim?"

I smiled and said, "I still haven't even met the man."

"Okay you two, why were you at Harold's church waiting for him?"

"Harold was concerned about some threatening notes he got telling him to get out of the Santa business." Trapper let that sink in. "I was going to help find out who was threatening him."

"The mob, maybe? Maybe Mickey Collisi threatened him and Harold decided to take care of the situation."

"Look, Deacon, believe me when I say Harold wouldn't murder anyone. He's too much of a wuss to kill anyone. I've known him since I was a beat cop on the strip. The worst he could do is annoy people with his preaching. Lynn, you were a cop around the city back then, you must have come across him?"

"Will, I don't remember you being around back then, let alone this Harold person."

"Street preacher, stood on corners telling people about his church on Industrial and Sahara. His father was Oscar Renford."

"Oscar Renford? He was his father. I remember good old Oscar. He would throw lavish parties and we'd get calls for peace disturbances. Harold is his son? I thought Oscar was gay?"

"Doesn't mean he couldn't have a son. When Oscar died, Harold got the building on Industrial and just about all of the property around there. Harold could be worth a lot of money if he sold out."

Lynn finally had a light go on. "Ah, I remember now. He used to go into casinos to tell people that gambling was evil. The casino security would escort him out and call us to move him along. Okay, he's a whack job, but was harmless, as I remember."

"Well, someone is going to great lengths to incriminate your friend if he didn't kill Collisi," Deacon said. "I see money involved with the property Harold owns, maybe someone wants it and figures on putting Harold away to get it."

"Take my word for it, Harold didn't do this," Trapper said.

I figured that Trapper wasn't going to explain about Harold and his affair with the wife of a major player in the casino business as an alibi. I just stood looking dumb.

"Pretty sure of yourself, I think you know more than you're telling," Deacon said.

"I got nothing, sorry. Now if you'll excuse me, I have to go call Sam and see what she wants to do tonight." He turned to the glass doors to our offices and went out of the lobby.

Deacon looked at me. I smiled and said, "I have Christmas gifts to get for Penny, I'll see you all later." I shot out of the lobby and ran into Trapper at the back by Fred's new room. He was talking to Fred at the door to his room.

"Do you remember him?" Trapper was asking. I presume it was about Harold.

"Sure, most street people knew Preacher Harold. I went to his church a couple times, it was a nice service. Then he would feed us. Nice guy. Is he in trouble?"

"It looks that way. Since you have a connection in the past to the New York mob scene, did you know a Mickey Collisi?"

"Collisi, sure. He was a pissant little hood who took over one of the mobs out in New York, after he rubbed out the reigning boss. I was asked to join his family, after I left Angelo's family when they were breaking up. I didn't like Collisi, so I came out here to Vegas to get away from the families back there."

"Well, Collisi was murdered today in a restaurant by a Santa they say was Harold."

"Gunned down in a restaurant, just like the old days." He smiled, thinking back.

"We need to find the real killer to get Harold off suspicion of murder."

"Anything I can do to help, just ask. I've been away from the mob scene for a long time, while I was homeless. But I could talk to Angelo and we can see if there was a hit put out on Collisi. That may help Harold," Fred said.

"That would be a start. Then we could track down the killer if we have a clue as to who it is," Trapper said.

"Fred, use the phone in my office to call Angelo," I said. "But, it's important to keep this quiet, we don't want the police to know anything."

"No problem, I'll call right now and get this rolling." He went to my office and in, closing the door.

"Crazy how he and Angelo found each other all these years later," Trapper said.

"If Fred hadn't found Willy that day he was dognapped, Fred would have never known Angelo was in the same city. Everything works out for a reason."

Fred came back out a few minutes later as Trapper and I were talking. He came to us and said, "Angelo is going to call back home to see what he can find out about Collisi's murder. Although Angelo said everyone wanted to see Collisi dead."

Chapter 6

"That's comforting to know," I said.

We turned to see Lynn coming through the doors from the front and down the hallway. I decided to just stand still. It would look suspicious to suddenly move away.

She came up to us and said, "I love Deacon, and I'd like to see him do good in homicide, but I think you two are holding something back from him."

I looked to Trapper and he smiled. "Let's go into my office. Fred, you can join us. May as well see what we do here."

The four of us went into Trapper's office across the hall from Fred's little living area. Trapper asked us to sit. Lynn pulled a chair over to the desk next to where I sat. Fred sat back by the wall.

"So, what do you suspect?" Trapper asked Lynn.

"Deacon left, and you know I'm on your side, even if you broke a few laws. You're hiding a suspect. Why?" she said.

Trapper hesitated, looked to me and I nodded. "Because Harold didn't do it."

"Okay, your proof?"

"He was with a woman when the murder of Collisi occurred." Trapper wasn't giving out much info.

"And the woman is?" Lynn asked.

"The wife of some big shot in the hotel community. He, Harold, didn't want to give her up. We don't know who she is," Trapper said.

"I think I know," I said. Lynn craned her neck towards me as did Trapper. "Harold said in the car that he met her at a charitable event and she was a chairperson for the soup kitchen. Penny and I contribute to that charity and the only woman on the board that I know of is Lila Westeen."

"You're just mentioning this now?" Trapper asked.

"You didn't ask my opinion," I defended myself.

"Westeen? As in Ben Westeen, the major player on the board of every corporation investing in Las Vegas?"

"I'm guessing now, Harold didn't say outright. But, it boils down to her," I said.

"Okay, Harold was with Lila, and Ben doesn't know. Not a good thing for Harold," Lynn said.

"That's why Harold couldn't use her as an iron-clad alibi. So he looks guilty," I said.

"You could have trusted Deacon with this."

"We just got back and didn't know what to say or what mood Deacon was in," Trapper defended.

"Okay." She got up and went to the door and waved down the hall. I could hear the glass doors to the front open and close. A few moments later, Deacon came to the door. Lynn pushed him back away from the door and we could barely hear them talking. Lynn was probably explaining the basics of what we said to Deacon, and he was not happy. Or, so I gathered from the tone of their voices. Lynn got loud and threatened Deacon, that part I could hear. He shut up and they both came in the room.

I could tell he wasn't happy, but he was calm. "Okay, truth on the table. What's the story?" he asked.

Santa Murders

Trapper went back over the whole sordid affair, from seeing Harold in his car on the street to delivering him to a friend. Trapper wasn't giving any information about Gus. Either protecting Gus or Harold. I didn't know.

"So, you took a suspect out of the city and hid him away. And you aren't going to tell me where?" Deacon asked.

"That's about it, right Jim?" he asked me.

"I'd say that was the whole story, well almost all of it," I said.

I could tell he was holding his breath when Lynn whacked him on the back. He exhaled and looked to us. "Okay, I would appreciate your devotion to me if I was in the same situation. Now you have to prove Harold didn't do this, with or without breaking any more laws, which you already have done. I'll give you two days before I arrest the both of you for obstruction of justice." He looked serious, then I could see his mouth crinkle a little. "I hate the both of you for not confiding in me. Trapper, you should know better. You were my superior officer out in Michigan, you would have never tolerated this, I'd expect better of you. And Jim, how many times did I save you from the attacks by Penny's cat?"

I broke out laughing and that killed the tension. We all started to relax. Fred was sitting quietly, probably wondering what we were all talking about.

"Seriously, guys, I would have listened if you told me earlier," Deacon said.

"We didn't have all the facts then, that's why we wanted to talk to Harold before the police got him. You guys never listen to reason, you suspect the first person involved. I knew Harold couldn't have done this. Right now the mob is possibly after him because the police made a big deal out of suspecting Harold, so they will be looking for him. He's hidden away safely."

Deacon was silent for a moment, "Okay, keep him hidden until you can find the real killer. I'll stall off the blood hounds and give you a little space to breathe. Don't disappoint me again, I'm not that hard to get along with."

We all agreed and stood to go out. Deacon stopped Trapper and me at the door. "You think Fred and Angelo can find out who this killer was? I mean, it looks like it was a professional hit on a mobster."

I turned to Fred standing behind us. "Let me know as soon as Angelo gets back to you. Do you have a cell phone?"

"Us former homeless people rarely have use for cell phones. It's not like I would call my friends in the tunnels to see how they're doing," he said with a smile.

"Not acceptable. You are part of our family now and I'll get you a cell phone to carry. That way I can bother you more often," I said with a laugh.

He grinned and I turned back to Deacon. "I'll be sure to let you know what Angelo finds out."

"Good, keep me in the loop. I don't want a mob war going on here. I'll talk to OCU and see what they may have under investigation regarding the local mobs."

"Maybe check with LA OCU and see if something is spilling over out here," Trapper offered.

"Nothing much left to do until we hear from Angelo, so I'm taking Fred to get him a phone. We may go by Angelo's restaurant to visit," I said.

"Don't forget to let me know. I can still arrest the two of you, so don't forget it," Deacon said and left us.

Trapper looked to me and said, "That didn't hurt too badly."

"Only Deacon's faith in us. We have to make it up to him by taking down a big crime in his name. Make Weber love him."

"Works for me, I'll wait for your call. I just may pay Lila Westeen a visit." Trapper left his office as Fred and I stood there.

"Okay, let's go shopping for a phone," I said to Fred. "Oh, and don't tell my wife I took you shopping." I walked out of Trapper's office and right into Penny, standing just outside the door.

"Don't tell me that you're taking Fred shopping? What else are you hiding from me? A mistress?"

"Uh, right now I think it would be safe to ask if you'd like to go shopping with us?"

"Yes, for your safety, that would be good to ask. Now let's go."

*

Chapter 7

Heading out to my car, I said, "You do know that I'm taking Fred to get a cell phone. That's all."

"Great, he needs one. But I'm going to take him shopping for some more new clothes."

"Penny," I said stopping her. "We have a situation that requires me to be ready to go save Santa at any minute. Fred is waiting for Angelo to call about a hitman, which is why we need to get a cell phone for him."

She was munching on the thought and then smiled, "Okay, go get him the cell phone, but when you get the info from Angelo for your case, I get Fred to myself." She smiled and went back into the building.

I was amazed by this woman and her cavalier attitude. Nothing seemed to bother her, she took everything in stride. I looked to Fred and said, "You poor man."

We drove out to a T-Mobile store I found on Google and got Fred a simple Android phone. He was assigned a number and I had him call Angelo to give him the number. Angelo had nothing to tell him yet, he said he'd call when he found out something.

We went back to the office and I found Penny in the lobby with Lacey. She saw me and said, "Are you done with Fred yet?"

"Not yet, I'll turn him loose when we get some info."

"I'll be waiting," she replied.

Trapper came out from the back and over to me. I said, "I thought you were going to see Lila Westeen?"

"I was. I had to track her down. That woman is busy. She has a personal assistant who keeps track of her movements and I had to book a time to talk to her. I can't see how Harold found a moment to meet with her."

"Well, I hope she made time for him while Collisi was being murdered. Or we're in trouble."

Trapper smiled and asked, "Feel like going along?"

"Sure. I just need to give Fred my cell phone number to call me if Angelo calls." I went back to Fred who was standing by Penny as she was talking

49

his ear off about where she wanted to take him shopping. Poor bastard.

"Fred, I'm going out with Trapper. Give me your phone." He handed me his phone and I programed my number in it. Then I explained how to call me and finished up with him.

He smiled and said, "I can't believe it, less than a month ago I was homeless and living in the storm tunnels. Now, I have a home and a cell phone. I have arrived."

I laughed, said he definitely had arrived, turned to Trapper and said, "Shall we go?"

Trapper drove his jeep to a building on Flamingo by South Jones Boulevard and parked in the lot next to it. We went in through the very ritzy vestibule decorated with thick carpet and Dutch style furniture. We approached the receptionist and Trapper introduced us, telling her we had a meeting with Mrs. Westeen.

The girl looked at the appointment book and then to the clock on the wall. "She'll be with you shortly. Please have a seat in the waiting area."

We went to the waiting room, but didn't bother to sit since our appointment was minutes away. Those minutes led to more minutes and then into a half hour. Trapper was getting really impatient and went back to the desk.

"Look, my time is as valuable as Lila Westeen's is. When is she going to honor our appointment that was supposed to be forty minutes ago?"

The girl looked flustered and made a call on her desk phone. She was holding her hand over the mouth piece and then hung up. "I'm sorry, but Mrs. Westeen is busy right now."

Trapper's neck was turning red. I knew what that meant. "Bullshit!" he called out loud. Then he went to the doors leading to what I presumed were the offices. I followed, mostly to keep him out of trouble.

He stopped a girl moving down the hallway. "I'm sorry, but I'm lost. Where is Mrs. Westeen's office?"

The girl smiled and pointed to a door at the end of the hall. Trapper thanked her nicely and we continued on our warpath.

He went through the door and found another receptionist. He didn't even bother to talk to her, he went through a door I'm sure was Westeen's office. I still followed.

Santa Murders

Lila Westeen was sitting behind a large desk talking to some man in an expensive suit. He looked shocked by our intrusion.

Trapper moved forward and took out his ID with the PI badge and flashed it quickly. I'm sure neither Lila nor her guest could see it properly. They probably thought he was a cop.

"Lila Westeen?" he spoke as the visitor sat quietly. "I need to talk to you about Harold Renford."

I could see that she was shaken by his statement.

"I was told I could talk to you fifty minutes ago. I have no time to wait around for you. A man's life is at stake."

Trapper looked to the man in the chair and smiled. "Sorry to break up your meeting, but this is an urgent matter."

The man stood and told Lila he'd be back. Then he left the room. Lila stood behind her desk, she looked small next to the wooden behemoth..

"What the hell do you think you're doing?" she said coldly.

"Harold Renford." He waited for her to respond. "Are you going to deny that you know him?"

She remained calm and cool. "I know of him. What about him?"

"Would your husband like to know you are playing pussy foot with him?"

That seemed to unnerve her a bit. She said, "Sit down and we can talk this through."

"Much better." Trapper sat and I followed his lead.

"Earlier today when Mickey Collisi was being killed in the lounge at the Venetian Hotel around noon, you were visiting with Harold Renford, correct?"

She sat quietly, analyzing what Trapper had just said. Trapper left her an opening, not saying they were doing the horizontal mambo.

"Maybe I was. Who is this Collisi you mentioned?"

"A mob boss, and it looks like Harold may have bumped him off. You're his alibi. I hope you'll do your civic duty and tell the police that Harold was visiting with you. Maybe we can spin it so your husband doesn't know the real reason for his visit."

She sat back in her expensive leather desk chair and smiled. "I appreciate your candor. Yes, I had a meeting with Harold around that time. He was with me discussing plans for a Christmas party for my husband. I like to have a big party for Ben just before Christmas and Harold is good at planning the thing. Being as he is a Santa and knows the right people to hire for the party. Now why is Harold being suspected of murder?"

"Well, a Santa went into the lounge and shot Collisi once, killing him, then fled. But before he left he threw a bunch of church flyers around. That's how the police identified him as the perpetrator."

Trapper took out a small digital recorder and said, "Now, if you could just state that Harold was with you, we can eliminate him from the suspect list."

She sat looking at the recorder. Then said, "I'm sorry, but I don't know what you're talking about. I haven't seen Harold Renford in over a week."

*

Chapter 8

"What the…" Trapper exclaimed. "You just said you were with Harold. What's going on?"

"I'm not sure what you mean, I never told you I was with Harold. I know the man, but I don't associate with his kind. Now, if you'll excuse me, I have business to attend to."

Trapper was just about coming out of his chair when I grabbed his arm. "Let it go," I said. "We need to let Mrs. Westeen go about her business."

Trapper was glaring at me as I stood and pulled him to the door. I said quietly, "Hang on, I have something to show you."

We were out in the lobby when he got really pissed. "How could she do that to Harold?"

"Well, he did say he came to tell her it was over between them. But that's not the good news," I said as I removed my Samsung Note 3 cell phone from my shirt pocket. I turned it on and clicked on the video icon. I found the file and played it for Trapper. It was our whole conversation with Westeen on video. Trapper was amazed and smiled. "Sometimes, you are so creepy."

"I started this when we went in and put it in my shirt pocket. The lens of the camera sticks above my pocket so it's easy to record anything in front of me. We only have to show this to Deacon to get Harold off the suspect list."

"I'd kiss you, but not in public," Trapper said.

"Or in private," I added.

He grinned and we left the office. We were back in the car when Trapper's cell phone buzzed. He looked at the caller ID and said, "It's Gus. I hope everything is all right." He answered and put it on speaker. "Gus, what's up?"

"Trapper, Harold is gone," said Gus through the phone speaker.

"What do you mean gone? He left?"

"Not sure, after you left, I heard him talking to a woman he called Lila, but I didn't hear all of it. Then later, he just vanished. I don't think he walked away. I took my fastest horse out to look for him, but didn't see him. I'm sorry, Will. I tried to watch him."

"It's okay Gus, I know you did your best. He's probably heading back here, but if you hear from him, call me and sit on him. Or tie him up. Thanks." He disconnected the call and sat looking miserable. "He doesn't know that we have the proof he's innocent."

"Gus said he talked to Lila. She didn't mention it," I said.

"Yeah and she didn't seem worried that we'd find out he did call her. Sort of like maybe she knew he was missing from us. I have a feeling Harold was taken."

Trapper's phone buzzed again, it was Gus. Trapper put it on speaker and said, "Gus, did you find him?"

"No, but I was outside when I called you and just now found an extra set of tire tracks coming up to the house, besides yours. Someone picked up Harold."

"Or kidnapped him. Thanks for that. Let me know of any more changes." He disconnected again. "Well, this is getting interesting. First, someone tries to frame Harold for murder, then they kidnap him."

Now my phone buzzed and caller ID said it was Deacon. "Aren't you glad we have cell phones," I said to Trapper with a grin. I put Deacon on speaker. "Deacon, what's up?"

"I just tried calling Trapper but got his voice mail, I didn't leave a message because I figured he was with you."

"He is and listening to us. What's going on?"

"We have Harold. He was dropped off a little while ago by two concerned citizens who left before we could get their names. Suspicious I'd say, but Harold is in custody."

"Well, don't do anything with him yet, not until we get there. Jim and I have an interesting tale to tell," Trapper said.

"Okay, but get here quickly before we'll have to book him. I'll stall it for now." He hung up.

"I think someone was trying to accelerate Harold's arrest," I said and put my cell phone away.

"Someone was worried that with Harold on the loose, it may mess up someone's plans. Let's go bail out Santa."

We drove over to Deacon's precinct and went in. We found Deacon in his office reading some papers. He smiled as we entered.

"I had Harold put in holding until I can do the paperwork on him. It takes me a while to do paperwork, so he's cooling his boots. Now, what is this earth shaking news you have?"

Trapper and I sat as I pulled my cell out again. I said, "We visited Lila Westeen to verify Harold's alibi, but after she told us she was with Harold during the shooting, she started to deny it. I have it on video."

I played the whole visit for Deacon, he enjoyed the show. "Good quality on that," he said. "I'll have Harold out in a few, just have to finish the paperwork."

"You really enjoy paperwork don't you?" I said with a laugh.

"Can we see Harold? I need to find out what happened to him and how they found him," Trapper said.

"Simple, he told Lila where he was when he talked to her," I replied. "She has to be in on it, otherwise, as you said, how could they find him?"

"Let's go find out. Can you get us in to see him?" Trapper asked Deacon.

Deacon yelled out to Warren in the squad room, and when Greg came up, Deacon told him to take us to see Santa. We left the room and went to the holding cells where we found Harold looking despondent. He cheered up when he saw us.

"Will, are you here to bail me out?" he asked as he stood up from the bench.

"We got you off the charges, we provided proof that you were with Lila when Collisi was murdered," Trapper told his friend.

"How'd you do that?"

"Long story. My friend Deacon is doing the paperwork to get you released, so be patient. Now, I need to know how you ended up here. Who took you from Gus' place?"

"I was on Gus' porch, he was in the barn doing something with his horses when this car drove up. I went to the car to see if you might have sent them. They got out and said they were investigators and the police sent them. They had guns, so I didn't argue. I was thrown in the back and told to shut up. They brought me here and dumped me. Your cop friend came and took me to this cell."

"Harold, I never told anyone where you were. It had to be Lila. Did you tell her?"

Harold thought on what he had said, "I guess I did say where I was, and also described the farm.

But why would Lila turn me in? She knew I was with her when the murder occurred."

I felt the presence of someone behind me, I jumped when I looked back and saw it was Deacon. "That's what we need to investigate," Deacon said to us. "Why Lila Westeen lied about a number of things." He looked to the jailer and said, "Cut him loose."

The four of us went back to Deacon's office and sat. Deacon had me copy the recording from my phone to his computer.

"Now, this whole case is getting confusing," Deacon said. "Some Santa murders Collisi and frames Harold for the job. Then, you two hide Harold away—which I'm not forgetting—but then you verify his alibi with Westeen, and now she's going to deny it, setting Harold up to take the fall. Harold talks to Westeen and he is grabbed by some men and brought here. Sure sounds to me like Westeen is involved."

*

Chapter 9

"I can't believe she would do this to me," Harold said, sounding crushed. "She told me she loved me."

"After knowing you for only a couple weeks? I've heard there's love at first sight, but that's hard to swallow," Trapper said. "No offense Harold, but you're no George Clooney."

"I know I'm not handsome, but she loved my charm and wit, she said."

"Harold, again, no offense, but since I've known you, you have no charm or wit. I'm sorry, but I can't buy that she loved you so quickly."

"I know Will. I was trying to believe it myself. It was great to have a beautiful, powerful woman romantically involved with me."

"Did she know who you were? The heir to Oscar Renford?" I asked.

"I told her, but I didn't think it meant much. I only got the buildings and property from my father.

The rest of his money went to people who didn't deserve it. But, not much I could do about that."

"Still, Harold, the property alone is worth a fortune for future development in that area. There are hotels and casinos going up all around you. Has anyone asked you if you wanted to sell your property?"

"Oh, many times, but I couldn't sell, that place is my home and my church is open to many people who need it. Where would they go?"

"With the money you'd get, you could build a better church. You could replicate the Crystal Cathedral out in Garden Grove, California. You could even do television sermons," Trapper said. "Reach a bigger audience."

"I like the ones I have now. Am I free to go?" he asked Deacon.

"You've been exonerated of all charges. But, be careful and stay nearby, there's still some reason for you being framed." Deacon looked to Trapper and me, "I think you should keep an eye on him until this is solved."

"I agree. I may need to call in a few markers on this, for his protection," I said.

"Who are you thinking of?" Trapper asked.

"Angelo."

"I think getting the mob in to protect a man accused of killing a mob boss may be risky," Deacon said.

"Fred said that Angelo told him there were many who wanted Collisi dead, and if we spread the word that Harold has been cleared of the charges, he may not have to worry about trouble from the mob. My concern is the persons who set this up. So Harold will need protection if it's about his property."

Deacon sat back in his chair and said, "Just keep me informed so we don't go shooting the wrong people."

"Well, Harold, shall we depart this place and go back to your church? We can swing by and pick up your car while we're at it," Trapper said.

"I have a murder to solve, I would appreciate any information you get," Deacon asked.

The three of us stood and we agreed to keep Deacon informed. We left the building and headed back to Trapper's Jeep. We drove over to the strip mall where Harold's car was still parked and Trapper told me to drive it. He told me quietly that he didn't want Harold to wander away.

We got back to the church and parked, went in, and there was a small group of people who saw Harold. They all got excited and came to us. Most of them looked like they were street people, homeless ones like I met when we first found Fred.

"Harold, they told us the cops were looking for you for murder," one man said.

Trapper stepped into the group and said, "Whatever you heard has been cleared up. Harold didn't murder anyone. We proved he didn't, so don't go spreading any rumors."

Harold spoke, "Thanks everyone, for worrying about me. My friends here helped me get over this mess and it's back to normal here in the church. Now we need to plan a Christmas party for the followers."

He led them all off to the back where they had a table set up with decorations and stuff for a party. Trapper smiled and said, "I hope Harold will be all right, but call your markers in anyway. Just to be sure."

"I'll call Angelo and see what he can get started." I went to the chairs again and sat, pulling out my cell phone. I called Angelo and he answered with a big hello. "Angelo, have you heard anything about Collisi's murder yet?"

"No, Mr. R, I got feelers out on it and will let Fred know what I find. What can I do for you?"

"I need to protect Santa, you still have any pull with any muscle around Vegas?"

"I do. You want wiseguys or just leg-breakers?"

"Leg-breakers will do, no deaths please. Just protect the man from harm. I've told Deacon about my plan and he's good with it, as long as there's no gun play, if possible."

"I'll get on it, where do they go and who do they see?"

I gave him the directions and Harold's name. I said, "Trapper and I will wait around a while, until your guys get here."

"I'll get them right over, don't you worry." He hung up. I didn't mind that, it meant he was on it.

I told Trapper what Angelo said.

"Good, now we need to confer with Deacon about what to do with Westeen. I'd like to see them drag her in for questioning. That would fix her snide butt."

Bob Moats

We watched Harold and his people putting up Christmas decorations as we waited. Harold put his spare Santa suit back on for the occasion. About a half hour later, two very big men entered and asked who Jim Richards was.

"That would be me. Did Angelo send you?" I asked.

"He did. He said you wanted us to protect Santa?"

I smiled and pointed to Santa. They both grinned, one man said, "I thought Angelo was pulling our leg. You is serious."

"Serious as a paper cut. I'll explain." I told them both everything from the frame job for murder to Harold's kidnapping and release from jail.

"Someone may still mess with Harold, so we need him watched to be sure he is safe," I said.

"With us, no man or woman shall bother his white beard."

I felt good now that we could leave Harold with the bruiser two. Trapper was ready to leave, as was I, it had been a long day.

Santa Murders

"I need to go home and see what Penny is up to and get some sleep. This is getting tiring, running around looking for killers."

"Yeah, I don't want to wear you out, at your age you should take it easy."

"Don't start about my age. I'll see you in the morning." I started to go to my car but realized it was at Trapper's apartment. "Okay, I have to put up with you a little longer," I said, and we went back to his place. I got my car and drove home.

Penny's car was in the garage and I was expecting her to start throwing Christmas paper at me and forcing me into wrapping gifts. I entered the house and it was quiet. I went to the living room and didn't find her. I tried the bedroom and she wasn't there either. Now I was worrying. I went to the spare bedroom and found Penny sound asleep on the bed with Willy by her side, surrounded by boxes. I decided to let her sleep and I went to our bedroom to see if I could sleep also.

*

Chapter 10

I didn't know what time it was when I was awakened by something hitting my body. I opened the one eye not sunk into the pillow and could see Penny in the light of the bathroom, whacking me with a roll of wrapping paper.

"You should have wakened me so we could wrap gifts," she said loudly.

"Babe, there's still a whole month before Christmas. We can do it this weekend." I sunk both eyes into the pillow, trying to get back to sleep. She whacked me again. I groaned and turned over to face her. "What do you want from me? It's too late to wrap now."

"Okay, but you are giving me a whole day to wrap, drink hot chocolate and roast marshmallows in the fireplace."

"You know I hate marshmallows," I said.

"That's your punishment. Now move over." She laughed and dropped her robe, she was au naturel. I knew a little French, she was naked. I knew I wouldn't be getting much more sleep this night.

Early the next morning, my cell phone buzzed on the nightstand. I opened one eye and saw it was just before eight. I reached over and grabbed the phone and answered. "Who is this?"

"Jim, it's Trapper. When you coming in?"

I buried my head back in the pillow and said, "Suck on it," and hung up.

I reluctantly got up and dressed, then prepared for work. Penny was already out the door, but she left Willy behind. I didn't ask why, just gathered his purse and took him with me. Besides, he needed to be with another dog and Fred's dog Henry would keep him busy.

I arrived at the office and Fred was out cutting the grass with the new lawnmower. He waved to me and I saw Henry tied to the back of the building. I smiled and went in. I put Willy on the floor and he shot off toward the front, probably to see Lacey.

I stopped at Trapper's office and he was relaxing at his desk.

"Man, you are a grouch in the morning," he said.

"Before eight, I am. Now, what was so important you had to wake me?"

"I talked to Deacon and they are putting Lila Westeen on the list of suspects involved in the murder of Collisi. He's going to send a couple detectives to bring her in for questioning. Since we know details that he doesn't, he said we could join him in questioning her. I got a few words for her."

"Now don't be rude, it'll only piss her off," I said.

"I'll piss her off all right. Deacon said they would have her in by nine, after her office opens up. Actually, I'd like to see her reaction when they do pick her up."

I heard a commotion and turned to see two small furry bodies fly past the door. I smiled as Fred came up. "Those two need more exercise," he said grinning.

"Keep an eye on them, so they don't get too rough. I presume you haven't heard from Angelo about the hitman?"

"No, I figured on calling him after I finished the lawn. I'll let you know."

"Thanks Fred," I said as he went off. I had to say, the dogs didn't make much noise barking, but I could hear them thumping around. It was good to see Willy playing with his own species. He had only known humans, which wasn't a good thing.

My cell phone buzzed and I took it out, it was Deacon. "Hey, big guy, what's up?" I put him on speaker so Trapper could hear.

"Have you talked to Will yet?"

"He's right here listening."

"Okay, I'm going with Warren to pick up Westeen, if you two would like to come."

Trapper yelled to my phone from his desk, "You bet we'd like to come."

I could hear Deacon laugh, "Okay, meet us at her office in fifteen. We'll wait for you." Then he hung up.

Trapper stood and grinned, "Let's go get the barracuda."

I told him I would let Lacey know we were leaving and went up front. I was surprised to see Willy and Henry both sitting quietly on the floor in the waiting area looking up as Lacey was standing over them.

"Now, I have rules here in my lobby. You both behave or I'll lock you in the break room." She was being firm with them. I had thought before that Lacey could communicate with animals. The way they both sat there listening to her confirmed my belief.

She turned to see me and said, "Got to put down rules or all hell will break loose."

"It's your lobby. Trapper and I are leaving to go bring in a suspect. We'll be back later. Oh, any messages for me?"

She just laughed, so I took that as a no. She turned back to the dogs and was giving them more rules as I went back to Trapper. He was waiting for me and was in a rush. We left and drove over to Westeen's office building. Her husband, Ben Westeen, probably had it built to keep her happy, or away from his offices.

We met with Deacon and Greg Warren as they were standing by the unmarked car. There was one patrol car nearby, probably to transport Westeen. Trapper and I went to the men and said our good mornings.

"Okay, you two have been here already, so you know the set-up. Lead the way," Deacon said.

Santa Murders

I could tell Trapper was enjoying this as he headed towards the front entrance. We went in and Trapper went straight to the door to the offices, passing the receptionist who sat with her mouth open.

Down the hall, we arrived at the inner lobby for Westeen's office and Trapper went past the secretary, not saying a word. He went through the door into her office and we found her at her desk on the phone. Trapper strode up to her desk, her eyes got wide seeing all the men enter the room. Deacon came around Trapper and stood next to him.

"Harriet, I'll get back to you, I have intruders." She hung up and stood. "What the hell is the meaning of this?"

"I have here, a warrant for your arrest for conspiracy to murder one Mickey Collisi." He signaled to the officers as they went around, putting the handcuffs on her. She was screaming, "You can't do this! I have my rights! I'll sic my husband on you and he'll have all your jobs!"

Deacon said, "He can have my job. I'm not fond of dealing with people like you. Take her out of here," he said to the officers and they led her out. She screamed to her secretary to call her husband.

We came out behind them and Trapper said to the secretary, "Please, by all means, call her husband. There are things he needs to know about her."

We went back to the cars. Westeen had settled down, seemingly because there were too many people in the main lobby for her to keep up the craziness. She was put in the back of the patrol car and we followed it to the precinct.

In the parking lot, Deacon told the officers to put her in an open interrogation room. They went in as Deacon turned to us approaching him.

"That felt really good," Trapper said.

"How soon can you get Harold back in here?" Deacon asked.

"I'll call and have him come in," Trapper replied.

"Do it and fast." Deacon went into the building while Trapper called Harold explaining the need for him to come in. He listened and then disconnected. "Harold said he'd drive right over. His body guards will be with him."

"When they get here, you should have the mob guys stay outside," I laughed.

*

Chapter 11

We went into Deacon's office. He was at his desk, standing with a folder in his hands. "I prepared a number of things we found out since yesterday. Sit." We did. "I had Warren run her financials and a large amount of money was deposited in her account then taken out the next day. Ten thousand dollars, maybe to pay a hitman?" He turned a page of the papers in the folder. "Last month, she placed a number of calls to a realtor and we contacted him. He said Lila Westeen had inquired about the value of the property owned by Harold Renford, and was interested in placing an offer to buy, under her company's name, 'Lila Investments,' So, it looks like she initiated the meeting with Harold deliberately."

"I wonder if her husband knew about her activities?" I asked.

"Hopefully, if her secretary got hold of Ben, he'll be in here and we can find out," Trapper said.

"Hopefully. It also seems that Lila filed papers for divorce on the grounds of his infidelity."

"Well, this just gets deeper and deeper for Lila," I said with a grin.

Warren came to the door and said, "Harold Renford is at the front desk. Want me to bring him back?"

Deacon said, "Put him in an interrogation room next to Westeen." Warren went off.

"Looks like the party is almost all here. Now we need Ben Westeen," Deacon said.

"He may bring his lawyer," I said.

"That will be good, especially if Harold brings up the fling he and Lila were having, her divorce might end up in his favor," Trapper said.

"I'm thinking that maybe Lila was going to buy the property from Harold and hold it over her husband. She wouldn't need his money then. Or, sell it to him for a huge amount. But if she was divorcing Ben, where would she get the money to buy the property?" I wondered.

"Good point to bring up. If we don't get too muddled in facts." Deacon stood and said, "Shall we go see what we have?"

We left his office and headed down to interrogations. We were standing in the observation room looking through the magic mirror into the two opposite rooms where Lila and Harold were sitting. Lila was looking quite mad.

The door to observation opened and Warren said, "Ben Westeen is here, with his lawyer."

"Good, the party is starting," Deacon said. "Bring him to this room, thanks Greg."

"We'll wait until Benny gets here and talk to him first." We waited about five minutes, then the door opened and in strode Ben Westeen with a suit following. He remained quiet while he looked at his wife in the other room.

He was calm and asked, "What has she done now?"

"Mr. Westeen, your wife is a suspect in a conspiracy to commit the murder of Mickey Collisi."

Westeen's head snapped back to Deacon and said, "Mickey Collisi? He's dead?"

"Yes, murdered yesterday by a person unknown. But the man in that room…" Deacon pointed to Harold, "was accused of the crime. During investigations by my office and these two private investigators, they determined that he was innocent because he was with your wife during the time of the murder."

Bob Moats

Ben looked at Trapper and me and asked, "Just what was he doing with my wife?" I could almost see a faint smile.

Trapper could hardly contain his excitement when he said, "We figured they've been dancing horizontally, based on what the man in that room told us."

"Do you have proof?"

Trapper continued, "We have your wife on video stating she was with him, but not saying what they were doing exactly. Although the man has claimed they were romantically involved. It's all hearsay, but looks incriminating."

Ben turned back to the one-way mirror and watched his wife, not saying anything. He turned to his lawyer and said quietly, "Start divorce proceedings immediately. I want the bitch to fry."

Deacon cleared his throat and said, "We also found out that your wife has already filed papers to divorce you for infidelity. Just recently."

Now he looked pissed. "Damn her. Sneaky little bitch. Get on it," he told the lawyer. The lawyer left the room.

"Do you know where she got ten thousand dollars recently, and what she did with it?" Deacon asked.

Ben turned back to Deacon, "She asked me for the money to use for her annual Christmas party. I thought it was a bit excessive, but she demanded it, as always. I have no idea what she did with it. Anything to keep her out of my business. What's the connection with Collisi?"

"You seemed surprised that Collisi was dead. Did you know him?"

He didn't speak right away, but then said, "If my wife had something to do with his murder, I'll tell you, but it's not for public consumption. I have investors to think about."

"Okay, tell us," Deacon said.

"I was in talks with a couple people about buying property on Industrial Road, south of Sahara. Collisi was one of them. He was going legit, breaking from the mob, and wanted to be the main investor. I don't have the liquid assets to buy the property, it's all tied up in investments, so Collisi made an offer I couldn't refuse. With him being dead, my deal may fall through."

"Did your wife know about this deal?"

He thought for a moment again, then said, "I had mentioned it in passing, but I didn't think she was interested in my business. She had her own pet projects."

"She also contacted a realtor about that property. She expressed an interest in buying. But if you don't know it, the man in the other room is the owner of the property. Your wife's lover."

Ben turned to the other mirror to look at Harold. "That man is the owner of the property I want? And my wife had him in her clutches? I hope she did murder Collisi, she'll fry for it."

"To get all this straight, your wife got a huge amount of cash from you, then did something with it, possibly hired a hitman. She inquired about the property that her lover owned. Collisi was murdered before he could help you buy that property. I'm seeing a thread here. I'd have to assume your wife was involved with the murder of Collisi to prevent you from buying the property. Does that make sense to you?" Deacon asked Westeen.

He didn't smile or frown, just stared blankly at his wife. "I shouldn't have married her. I felt she was trouble. But she was good in bed and knew how to butter me up. She pushed to get married. Lately, I had all my money tied up in investments, so her luxurious lifestyle wasn't as good as she wanted. I should have seen the divorce thing coming." He turned back to us. "This doesn't leave this room. There was someone who I was in love with long ago, but she was married. Recently, her husband died and we ran into each other at a party. One thing led to another and we had become involved. My pre-nup only stated that if Lila was unfaithful, she got nothing. It didn't say anything about me, but she could cause trouble with a good lawyer. This may help to speed up the divorce."

Deacon said, "Well Mr. Westeen, I'll see if we can help you and put her away for murder."

*

Chapter 12

"Don't be gentle, she can take it. She's meaner than she looks," Ben Westeen said.

"Okay, we're going in, just don't yell anything to the glass. We can hear you if you yell."

"I don't want her to even know I'm here, I want her to think she is all alone in this mess."

Deacon looked to us and motioned to leave. We went out and around to the door going into Lila's room. She jumped when Deacon forcefully opened the door. We all went to sit by the table she was at. They hadn't cuffed her to the table, I guessed they figured she couldn't do much harm against us.

"Why am I here and why are you delaying me? I have a business to run," she blurted out.

We let Deacon do all the questioning. "All in due time, Lila. We have some questions to ask. First, do you know Mickey Collisi?"

"I've heard of him as a member of some mob, I don't personally know him."

"Did your husband know him?"

"I don't think so. He would never deal with mob figures. He runs a legitimate business."

"You had in your bank account, a deposit of ten thousand dollars, what did you do with that?"

"How do you know what I have in my accounts, that's invasion of privacy."

"Not in a criminal investigation."

"Criminal? I've done nothing wrong."

"Just answer the questions and we'll see. What did you do with the ten grand and where did you get it?"

"I got it from my husband, it was for our annual Christmas party."

"Mighty expensive party for ten grand. How do you justify the expense?"

"There's a lot that goes into a party. Hell, parents spend more than that to marry off their daughters."

"Well, Lila, that may be true, but I think you used the money to pay a hitman to bump off Collisi."

"Are you insane? Why would I want Collisi murdered?"

"For starters, he was going to help finance your husband in buying property on Industrial by Sahara. Do you know this property?"

"No, I don't know what you're talking about."

"You became involved with Harold Renford, he's the owner of that property."

She looked to Trapper and me. "These two bozos asked me about this Redfern, I don't know him."

"It's Renford." I corrected as I leaned forward with my cell phone and said, "How's this from a bozo?" I played the video from where she admitted she was with Harold during the time of the murder.

"Where did you get that? That's illegal."

Deacon continued, "You got a large sum of money, whereabouts presently unknown. You also inquired about buying Harold's property with a real estate agency. Collisi was going to help buy the property for your husband, but he was murdered before he could. I'd say you have a lot to explain to the D.A. after we book you for conspiracy to commit murder."

"I want my lawyer," she said defiantly.

"Is that the same lawyer your husband uses? Because as of twenty minutes ago, he's busy filing papers for your husband to divorce you."

Her eyes grew and she yelled, "Is that son-of-a-bitch here? Benjamin, are you here? You slimy bastard." She was up out of her chair and went to the mirror and yelled, "Are you over there, you cowardly sleaze ball? I could tell things about your dirty dealings."

We could hear through the glass, a voice yelling, "Screw you, bitch."

I was trying not to laugh as Deacon got up and pulled Lila back towards the door where he told the cop just outside to take her to booking. He said he would send the paperwork.

Trapper and I got up and followed Deacon back to the observation room. Ben Westeen was already coming out. "You fry her good, you hear. Now, may I talk to Renford?"

"After we talk to him. Just go back in there and watch," Deacon said and Westeen went back in the room. Deacon sighed, "Sometimes I get tired of this."

I smiled and said, "I'm sure Buck's security guards could use you if you wanted to quit the force."

He gave me a dirty look and went to Harold's door and in. We followed, Trapper was laughing quietly to himself.

Deacon smiled and sat across from Harold. "Hello, Harold. We meet again. Just a few questions then we can have you back to whatever you were doing."

"Oh, I was getting ready for our Christmas party next week," he said.

"Next week, isn't that a little early before Christmas?"

"We always have it early, to give my people time to be with their families. Many of them are scattered around the city."

"That's good. Now, I need to know a few things. First, when did you meet Lila Westeen?"

"It was at a Thanksgiving party at her office. I was asked to come and play Santa."

"Who asked you?"

"I was told it was Lila's people. They knew I played Santa and they gave a generous donation to my church for appearing there."

"Good, now when did you personally meet Lila?"

"I was on a break at the party, and she came to me. We talked for a while, she seemed so nice and attentive to me. Then she asked if I would like to have lunch with her that week. I agreed. We met at Le Chic and had a nice lunch, then we went to an apartment she said belonged to her business. I was really liking this woman, and, well, one thing led to another."

I could just barely hear Ben on the other side of the mirror saying, "Damn bitch."

Deacon ignored the comment. "Harold, you have a great deal of property, have you ever considered selling it?"

"As I told Jim and Will, I want to keep the property. It was my father's when he started out in business. He had a box factory there, he made a fortune in boxes, then he started investing in property. He was making lots of money by selling the property to those wanting to build their hotels and casinos. Getting twice, and often three times what he paid for it."

"Has anyone approached you to sell?"

"Oh sure. Lots of times. I just tell them no. I got offers just last week from two different companies about selling. They offered lots of money, but I don't need it."

"What do you mean you don't need it?"

He leaned forward and said quietly, "I have lots of money stashed away." He grinned and sat back.

Trapper spoke now. "Harold, I've known you for years, you never said you had any amounts of money. Although, I did wonder how you paid taxes on the property."

"Will, I'm a man who lives modestly. I only use the money to take care of the property and occasionally make charitable donations. But I do it anonymously. I don't want them bugging me for more money.

"May I ask how much money you have?" Deacon asked.

"Don't tell anyone, but after I paid the taxes on it, I have just over three million dollars. See, I don't need to sell my property."

The three of us all looked at Harold in shock. Here's this man in old clothes and running a church for street people and the homeless, and he was sitting on three million dollars. I was totally blown away.

*

Chapter 13

Trapper closed his mouth then opened it long enough to ask, "Three million dollars? Harold, where did you get that kind of money? Did your father leave it to you?"

"No, I had a good amount of money from my younger days. It was money my grandfather left me when he passed on. He was my mother's father and he didn't like my father. Over the years, I invested it in a couple casinos and I still own a tiny percentage of them today. The money comes from them. I get a check quarterly and I just cash it and stash it. I don't tell people about it because I want people to like me and not my money. I know that my property is presently worth fifty-nine million dollars if I sold today, or more if I really worked a buyer. They all want that area for development. I'm not letting the property change from what it was when my father had it."

"Harold, the buildings are dilapidated and falling down. I'm surprised the city hasn't condemned them."

"It's not the buildings the buyers want. They'll just tear them down to build their hotels. If things get bad, I may sell."

"Okay, we know you have money, but we need to know about Lila. Did she ever say anything about the property?" Deacon asked.

"She asked about it once and I told her the same thing. I wasn't going to sell. She never said much more after that."

"Did you tell her you were rich?"

"No, I never said anything about that, not to her or anyone. Well, I told you guys, but I trust you."

I was thinking about Westeen in observation. I hoped he wouldn't go after Harold over the property and his money. "Harold, we need to talk after we're done here," I said.

"Sure Jim, anything for you."

Deacon stood and said, "I have nothing more to talk to you about. But, you'll probably be called to testify at the trial for your involvement with Lila. Don't let them fluster you."

"They can ask me anything, I'll tell the truth. I have nothing to hide, I didn't do anything wrong."

"Fine, I have no more to say. Trapper, would you see that Harold gets back to his church safely, do that quickly."

He turned and was heading out when I stopped him and said, "Would you please delay Ben Westeen from bothering us?" He agreed and left.

I went over to the switch on the wall that shuts off the speakers to observation and turns off the recording equipment. I lowered the blinds to cover the mirror and locked the door. I went back to sit next to Trapper.

"Harold, how you spend or keep your money is your business. But I'd like to make a few suggestions. You do very well to help the less fortunate in the city with your church, but how about going a little further."

Harold leaned on the table and listened. "What do you propose? I do care for the people and want to help."

I thought three million dollars could help a lot of people, but it wasn't my money.

I explained how we found the homeless living in the storm flood tunnels and about Fred's friend Henry dying during the last flood. Harold said he knew about the tunnels and tried to get people to leave them.

"Harold, that's great, but they have no place to go. You can't make them leave the only home they know, no matter how dangerous, without a solution. I have an idea. I know of a large motel that's for sale, I thought about buying it, but it was a little more than I could handle money-wise. It's been sitting for a while and I wanted to buy the motel and turn it into a shelter for the homeless. Setting up three or four persons in each room. That building is big enough and I figured it could take in over three hundred or more homeless persons. About as many as there are living in the tunnels. There's also a very big community room where you could hold your services. If it's something that might interest you, we could talk more."

He sat back and was thinking. "I'll let you know."

"Good. Now, you're going to be bugged by Ben Westeen, Lila's husband. He knows you own the property. He wanted your property and Collisi was going to help him to try and buy it. Westeen didn't have enough money so he turned to Collisi, but now that the mobster is dead, he may try something else to get your property. Just be on the lookout for him."

"Thanks," Harold said and we stood. Trapper said he'd get Harold back to his bodyguards.

"Do I need them now that they know Lila was behind it?" Harold asked.

"Harold, I'm not convinced this is all about Lila. There's still a hitman out there. So you still need protection."

He agreed and we took him out, bypassing Deacon's office figuring he had Ben in there talking about his involvement in this case.

We found Angelo's men outside sitting on Harold's car. They got in the car with Harold and we said our goodbyes. Harold drove off.

"Three million dollars and he sits on it. I always knew he had a gear loose," Trapper said.

"Will, it's his money and he can do what he wants. Because of my book sales, I'm almost a millionaire. I sit on my money, too. But I do donate, like Harold does. So he'll do what he wants with it. I just hope he uses it to help the people he's so concerned about."

"Maybe we'll have a Christmas miracle and he'll use it for good," Trapper said.

"One can only hope."

"You're not going to let this go, are you? You'll be bugging him with your ideas."

"No, I'm not. He'll come around on his own."
I made a sly smile and left Trapper.

We went to the car and drove back to the firm. I was singing quietly. "HARK! The Preacher Harold's rich, fa la la la la, la la la la. Westeen's plans are in the ditch, fa la la la la, la la la la."

Trapper roared out loud with a laugh as we arrived at the firm.

Fred was in the back with Willy and Henry each on a leash. I went over to them and said, "You could make a fenced in pen for them so they could run free. A dog run would be nice."

Fred looked around and smiled, "Yeah, it could be done."

"Maybe a good twenty foot run next to the building. I think that would give them fresh air and exercise. Plus, this side of the building is out of the sun so they wouldn't get overheated. Get Buck stoked up on the idea, he can help to set it up."

"I'll do that. Oh, your wife is in the building."

"Thanks for the warning," I said and went in. Trapper was already in his office looking at his computer. I went to the front.

Penny was talking to Lacey at her desk. The two were laughing, probably talking about me. Then they saw me and went serious.

"Fine, I know you were talking about me. I don't have a problem with it."

They both started laughing again. I just sighed and went back to my office.

*

Chapter 14

Trapper called to me from his office. I went there and in. "What's up?"

"I got a call from Harold, he's going back to bell ringing tomorrow at the mall. I told him he should take a break, but he's being bull-headed."

"Are the bouncers going to be with him?" I asked.

"He said they wouldn't let him out of their sight. Since they were sent by Angelo, I believe they'll be close by or have to deal with Angelo."

"I don't understand. Why doesn't Harold just fill the pot with money and call it a day? What is it with this man?" I asked.

"Jim, Harold is a pragmatist, he believes that he can do good by his actions and not his money. That would be too easy."

"So he figures to get others to help his plan by donating money to the cause, by dropping change in the pot?" I said.

"Yep, that's Harold. He won't take the easy way out."

"Okay, but with donations from his bell ringing, his way takes too long. People can starve to death before he gets enough money to feed them. It's just not right when he has so much money." I shouldn't have, but I was getting a little mad at Harold. "I wish I could knock some sense into him to do some good with his money." I went silent and Trapper didn't say anything. "Okay, maybe I'm being a little unfair. I know I have money, but I do donate, and so does Penny. I couldn't help everyone from the tunnels, but I got Fred out. I do what I can."

Santa Murders

I turned and went out of his office. Embarrassed that I didn't do more. I'd go visit Harold tomorrow at his place at the mall and give him a good donation that will help his people. I guess it was my way of making me feel good. And help a few more people. I left my office and went out to talk to Fred. I had another plan.

He and I talked while Willy and Henry bounced around on leashes staked into the ground. They were funny getting themselves all tangled up in the ropes. I told Fred about an idea, and he liked it. I told him we would talk more about it later, but before Christmas. He agreed.

I went back in and found Penny. I asked her to follow me to my office and she did. I told her my plan and she agreed. She said she'd talk to a few others she knew to see if they'd want in on the plan. She came over and kissed me, "I knew I kept you around for a reason. Shall we go home and celebrate our new venture?"

I didn't argue. I went to tell everyone we were leaving and gathered up Willy. I said goodbye to Fred, walked with Penny to our cars and we went home.

Sometime in the early morning, the sun wasn't even up yet, our house phone rang. I was getting weary of these early morning calls, but answered. It was Trapper and it was four in the morning.

"Jim, wake up. Harold is gone," he said in the phone.

I sat up shaking my head, "What did you say?"

"Harold turned up missing this morning. His bodyguards went to check on him and he wasn't in his room."

"Do they think he was taken, or just wandered off?"

"The back door to the church was forced and they think he was taken. The men called Angelo and he's getting a number of his people to the church to organize. Angelo called me. Your cell phone wasn't picking up."

"Okay, I'll meet you there," I said and hung up. I picked up my cell phone, it was shut off. I had to stop doing that in my sleep. I dressed, and Penny mumbled about what I was doing. I told her and she got up.

"You don't have to get up, babe," I said.

"It's Saturday morning, I don't work and I'm going in with you to see what's going on."

"Okay, but take your .38 with you, just in case."

She smiled and said, "You know that's an accessory I always take with me. I never leave home without it."

We were dressed and in my Crown Vic in 15 minutes. We left Willy sleeping in the bedroom, he'd be alright. We arrived at the church and the sky was just getting light from the sunrise. I rarely saw it and it was pretty. Trapper's Jeep was parked next to the building and there were a number of other cars in the lot. I figured they were Angelo's friends.

We went in and saw Trapper talking to a small group of men. Penny went to the coffee urns as I went to Trapper. Before I could even reach them, Deacon stormed into the building.

I turned to see him as he said, "Okay, someone talk to me."

Trapper went to him and explained the events of the morning. I was standing just outside the ring of people around Trapper and Deacon.

"Has there been any ransom demands or a note left here?" Deacon asked.

"No, neither. He just vanished. I checked the door and can see it was forced. Someone came in and took him."

Trapper looked around at all the men and said, "No one saw anything?"

"There were only two men with Harold at the time and they were taking turns watching him. But whoever came in went through a back way and down the side to Harold's room. The two men were out front here so they couldn't see them."

"This doesn't make sense. If he was taken for the property, no one would get it if he turned up dead. It would be seized by the government, unless he had a will."

"Or, they forced him to sign a new will," I offered. Penny came up to me and said the coffee was really bad. I smiled.

"Okay, there's not much to do. All of you men called by Angelo, call around to whoever you know that may have an ear to what goes on in the underworld. See if there was anyone hired to grab Harold."

All the men went off with their phones and were calling whoever they could. This would be an interesting morning for the mob.

Santa Murders

Deacon came over to me and Penny. "Are you slumming, Penny?" he said.

"Just wanted to watch the wheels of justice turn," she said.

"It will turn slowly, unless we get a break," Deacon said.

"Maybe you should check with Ben Westeen and see where he was tonight," I said. "I don't think he'd be part of the kidnapping, but he knew Harold was wealthy and owned the property he wanted. I'd say he'd be your first suspect."

"I'd have to agree. I'll call to have him brought in."

"He's not going to be happy this early in the morning," I said.

"He'll get over it, I didn't like the man." Deacon pulled his cell phone and called Warren. "I hate to wake up Greg so early, but it's part of the job," Deacon said with a smile.

He explained to Warren what he wanted and said he'd wait until Greg called. All of Angelo's men were conversing, but no one had any good news to tell.

"Someone wanted this property. There has to be a reason they deem important for them to take Harold."

I said, "Maybe Harold has his millions stashed away somewhere in this building. That would be motive enough to take him. Force him to talk."

Deacon said, "You, me and Trapper were the only ones who knew about his money. But Westeen heard it, too. I'm going with him for this."

*

Chapter 15

Greg Warren called twenty minutes later and told Deacon that according to someone at his office, Westeen was out of the country.

"Damn, he should know better than to leave with his wife facing criminal charges," Deacon said after telling Trapper and me what Warren told him.

"Maybe that's the point, he said he hoped that she would go down for the charges. Helps his divorce if she's in jail," I said.

Santa Murders

"Okay, I'll give him that. But to suddenly be out of the country this quickly. It looks bad for him." He still had Warren on his phone. "Greg, check with the airlines and verify that he left."

He hung up and looked around the room. "Okay, if Harold did hide his money here, and supposing the bad guys figured he did, where would it be?"

I turned to see Angelo's friends standing around drinking lousy coffee and talking. "You got a whole bunch of gangsters here who know how to make money disappear, why don't you have a scavenger hunt?"

Deacon laughed and called to the men. They came over and gathered around Deacon. "Men, I have a problem. The preacher of this church is missing, and it seems he may have money stashed away here. This could be the reason he was taken, to give up the location. If you all could spread out and see if you can find a possible hiding place, we can beat the kidnappers before they get the info."

One of the men spoke up, "What's in it for us?"

Deacon thought for a moment, "I'll give a pass on future charges, short of murder, that may come up for the man who finds the stash."

They all looked to each other and then went off in a hurry. Trapper said he was going to keep an eye on the hoods and went off. Deacon yelled, "Don't destroy the building!"

"This is a big building, bigger if you include the old box factory. Harold could have put it anywhere," I said.

Deacon smiled, "There are about fifteen of Angelo's friends searching, with incentive, we have all day. I'm sure it can't hurt to have them looking over all the buildings."

Penny was wandering around, looking at the posters and literature about the church. The papers all talked about how God from above was watching over us. She looked up and saw the skylight with a railing around a level just below the glass. It looked like a perch to observe the area below.

"Jim, Deacon, can you come here?" she said.

We went to her and she pointed up. "If Harold believed God from above was taking care of him and his flock, wouldn't it be a safe place to have him watch his money, too."

We were looking at the level above us. Deacon called to the assistant of the church and asked, "How do we get up there?"

The young man looked puzzled and said, "I don't know, I've never been up there."

"Okay, do you know of any stairs or openings that go up?"

He thought for a moment and said, "Yes, there is an old set of stairs that go to the attic, but Harold said never to go up there. It's was dangerous because the building was old and a person could break through the flooring and crash down here."

"Show us the stairs," Deacon said and the young man took us to a door on the side of the room. He unlocked the door with a key and opened it.

There was a stairway going up and it looked dilapidated. I turned to Penny, "You stay down here. I don't want you hurting yourself. You need to stay healthy for Willy."

"I don't want you hurting yourself either, so be careful," she replied.

Deacon turned to the young man and said, "What's your name?" The young man said his name was Joel. "Okay Joel, stay here and make sure no one else follows us."

The man nodded and waited with Penny while Deacon and I climbed the stairs. The steps creaked and groaned as we ascended. I was waiting for Deacon's huge body to go through one of the steps.

"Harold isn't a small man, so if he came up here, he made it safely," Deacon said.

"Or, he knows a safer way to go," I said.

"You're a real comfort, you know that?"

We got to another level that must have been the attic. Light was coming through the huge skylight above, helping us to maneuver around. I was amazed at all the things that would be considered antiques. Among them were sewing machines, clothes on racks and boxes marked 'dry goods'.

There had to be a fortune for antique treasure hunters up here. We moved around the level carefully as the flooring did creak and sag as we walked.

I pointed to another door on the side. Then I said, "Look at the floor. The years of dust have been disturbed by footprints coming from that door to that wardrobe." I pointed to a large ornate cabinet that probably once held clothing for someone.

We went to the cabinet, it was locked. Deacon found a shovel on a pile of machinery that may have been used to make something, though I didn't know what. He took the shovel to the cabinet and pried at the doors. The lock finally gave and he set the shovel down. He said to me, "If any creatures jump out, stop them." I knew he was referring to the Narnia books about the magic wardrobe. He opened the doors and we saw it. Piles of money, lots of it.

"Well, we found his stash," Deacon said.

"Thanks for saving us the trouble," came a voice from behind us. We turned to see Joel and Penny standing before two men with guns. Deacon and I didn't draw our weapons because of the hostages between us.

One man came around and smiled at seeing all the money. He called to someone back at the stairs, and two more men came up.

The lead man told them to get the money. The two men pulled out garbage bags and started to put the money in. Penny was still by the young man as the fourth man guarded them. She was holding on to her purse, where I knew she kept her Smith and Wesson .38 handgun. I hoped she was careful if she took it out. My Glock was in its holster and I didn't know if these men knew I had it.

"So, just who are you connected with?" I asked to distract them.

"None of your business. Just shut up and wait for us to finish," the lead man said.

"What? So you can kill us? I think not." I nodded to Penny as she drew her gun and spun around, shooting the man behind her. The lead man turned as Deacon pulled his gun and shot him. The two men gathering the money just held their hands up and surrendered.

Penny came to me, "You always make me save you by shooting someone."

"And I'm glad for it, babe," I replied and kissed her.

The two men who were shot were alive and Deacon had called for back-up. We tied up the men with ropes we found among the piles of stuff. Trapper came up and helped after we explained what happened. Angelo's men were coming up the stairs and Deacon told them to get back down to the main floor.

Penny and I were standing, looking at all the money in the cabinet. "This could be put to better use," I said, "than hiding it up here."

"You really need to have a talk with Santa," Penny said.

About twenty minutes later, Deacon's cops showed up and were taking the bad guys away. The two wounded men went off in an EMS unit. The other two were taken back to be interrogated.

Chapter 16

Deacon called Warren to come in with Williams and had them inventory the money being guarded by two officers. Penny, Trapper and I went back to the main floor and were waiting for Deacon to finish up. We were anxious to go interrogate the men to see were Harold was.

Deacon had the building cleared of all non-essential persons, and thanked the men who came in from Angelo's calls.

I looked to Trapper, "You know, Angelo could start his own little mob out here."

"What makes you think he doesn't already have one?" he smiled. I silently pondered that.

The money was counted, bagged and carried out by Williams, Warren and the officers, to be taken back to lock-up until we could find Harold. It was seen by too many people to leave it where it was. Warren said they counted about two and a quarter million dollars.

"Harold told us he had three million, so he either hadn't counted it lately or hid more around," I said to Deacon and Trapper.

"I'm sure he just wasn't keeping tabs very well. Harold wasn't very organized in that way," Trapper replied.

Harold's young assistant was told to lock up the building and take the day off. The building was now a crime scene. He looked upset, but did Deacon's bidding. We went back to our cars and over to the precinct.

The two men who were arrested were put in separate rooms and Deacon led us to observation. Penny went in and sat. I followed Deacon and Trapper to go talk to the first man.

He was looking antsy and jumped when we came in. Deacon had identified him by his driver's license and sat across from him. Trapper and I stood back and tried to look menacing. The man wasn't very tough looking, in fact he looked rather mousy.

"So Sammy, your buddies are in the hospital being treated for gunshot wounds. You were smart to give up before we might have shot you. Might have even killed you. Lucky one you are. Let's see how lucky you are to get out of this room alive." Deacon sneered at him. We could see Sammy cringe a little. "Now, I'm not saying I'll harm you, I'm a cop so I can't do that. The two men behind me aren't cops and they are friends of Angelo DeMarko. You've heard of Angelo, right?"

The man's eyes widened and he nodded slightly. "Good, if you aren't cooperative, I can just go for a long coffee break while they have a talk with you."

Now he looked panicky. "What do you want to know? I'm not good with pain." He was shaking a little.

"Well, Sammy, we are missing a friend by the name of Harold Renford. Do you know him?"

The man shook his head no, and said so.

"Okay, why were you taken to the church with your other buddies?"

"I was told to go with Luke, he's one of the men you shot, and to follow him. I wasn't told why. I just follow orders."

"Where did you start from? Before you came to the church?"

"We got a building over on Jones by Desert Inn. We have meetings there."

"What kind of meetings?"

"About things we need to do. Like muscling people into selling their homes for development. I don't get into the reasons why, I just follow orders."

"Okay, do you know Ben Westeen?"

"Never heard of him. But I've heard of some dame named Westeen. Can't remember her first name, it was strange."

"Lila?"

"Yeah, I think that was it. She wanted us to muscle some guy about selling his property to her."

"When did she ask this?"

"Just yesterday. Luke got a couple men and went out. I had other things to do so I don't know what they did."

"If they went to grab someone, would they have brought him to your building?"

"Yeah, I just got back this morning when Luke told me to grab some garbage bags and follow him. We got to that church and were going to a door when we found that kid and the dame standing by it."

"So, Luke knew where to go to get to the attic?"

"I guess so. He went right to the door. I guess he knew where to go."

Deacon turned to us and said, "They must have gotten Harold to talk. I'm sure they'll keep him alive to be sure the money was where he said it was."

Trapper said, "I just hope they didn't hurt him too badly."

Deacon turned back to Sammy. "Who's your boss?"

"I follow Luke, he's my boss. I don't know who Luke takes orders from."

Deacon stood and said, "You can cool your heels in lock-up for now. Until we find who we're looking for." He went out, followed by us, and told the guard at the door to take Sammy back to his cell.

"Are you going to talk to the other man?" Trapper asked.

Deacon thought. "I don't think we'd get better answers, but maybe he knows the people in charge. Okay, one more time." He went to the second room and in. This man's name was Steve and he sat looking smug.

Deacon didn't sit this time, but he leaned on the table and spoke to the man who was still looking cool and calm. "Steve, we already got most of the information we need from your man Sammy." That got Steve's attention, he looked up to Deacon, but still showed no emotion. "Do you know a man named Westeen?"

The man gave no indication of recognition. Deacon continued, "How about Lila Westeen?" Still no answer. "Look Steve, Sammy will most likely skate on charges easier than you if you don't want to cooperate. I just want to know who you take orders from."

Steve's eye were finally showing some life, he looked at Deacon, then us and said, "I don't know names, orders just come over the phone. I've had a few lieutenants from the organization come in to see if we were doing our jobs. They never said who they reported to."

"Organization? You are part of a mob? Whose?"

Steve paused and went silent. Deacon tried something again. "Steve, these two men behind me are good friends with Angelo DeMarko. I'm sure you know him. Now, I can have them ask you questions or you can just give me a couple names. What mob?"

"The Collisi family," he said quietly as if someone would hear him.

Deacon straightened up. "Collisi? Do you know he was murdered?"

"Yeah, I heard. It was someone in another organization who put out the hit so they could take over."

Deacon turned to us and spoke quietly, "This isn't making sense. If Collisi was helping Westeen to buy Harold's property, we thought Lila hired someone to bump off Collisi to mess up her husband. So who is this person who set the hit on Collisi so they could take over?"

He turned back to Steve, "You don't have a clue as to who may have set up the hit on Collisi?"

"If I say, and it comes out I did, I may as well make out my will."

"I'll see you get protection through the Marshall's Witness protection. Talk."

He hesitated, thought about it and finally said, "I don't know his full name, I heard they refer to him as Casino Ben."

*

Chapter 17

Deacon turned and took us out of the room, and told the guard to take Steve back to his cell. He stood in the hallway and was thinking. Trapper and I waited, and then Trapper said, "You realize that Ben Westeen owns casinos and the name Casino Ben is most likely him."

"Thanks for the news flash, Will, I kind of figured that out. I'm just puzzled as to why Westeen murdered Collisi, and whether or not his wife knew he was a mob boss? I'm trying to put the puzzle together. Maybe Lila didn't hire the hitman. But Sammy's boss said she requested Harold's kidnapping. She somehow got word out from her jail cell to them."

"Did Lila talk to a lawyer? Maybe he arranged it," I said.

Deacon smiled and headed out. I had to get Penny, and Trapper followed Deacon. I went into observation. Penny looked to me and said, "Is the show over? That wasn't very exciting."

"It was exciting for Deacon, let's go." She got up and we went out. I figured Deacon was going to see if Lila had any visitors and found him and Trapper standing by the front desk. He was looking at the entry log. He turned to us and said, "Lila had a visitor last night, a lawyer. His name is Benjamin Docktor. I don't know the connection of his name with the casinos, but he is a Ben."

"Check the log and see who came with Ben Westeen," I said.

Deacon looked down the list of visitors and found Ben Westeen. "Son of a gun. His lawyer is Ben Docktor. He played Westeen for a fool, he was working with Lila also."

"I'd say he's playing both of them. This shyster put the hit out on Collisi. He knows criminals so it would be easy for him to find a hitman," I said.

"Okay, Docktor doesn't know we suspect, so we need to rescue Harold, ASAP," Trapper said. "Before any of his people know we have the gang in custody."

"Yeah, let's take care of that. We can nab Docktor at our leisure." Deacon went back to his squad room and called to anyone available to go on a raid. I asked Deacon if he knew where we were going. He stood thinking.

"I'll get Sammy and take him with us. He knows." Deacon called over to Warren and had him follow. We waited and a few minutes later they came out with Sammy in cuffs. We went out to the cars where there were a good number of cops waiting to go.

Deacon and Warren took the lead car, with Sammy navigating. I presumed they made promises to him if he helped. I followed all the cops behind Deacon. Trapper drove over with Penny and me, no sense in adding more cars to the parade. We headed over to Jones and Desert Inn roads and then Deacon pulled into a building parking lot. He pulled up to a door and stopped. Everyone exited their cars. I told Penny to stay back for now, and then Trapper and I followed them.

I presumed Sammy had told him which door to hit and Deacon went through. Everyone followed him and Warren with weapons ready.

"I'm waiting to hear gunfire before I go in," I said.

"You'd make a lousy cop," Trapper said and rushed in. Oh hell, I figured with all those men in front of me, what chance would I have of being shot? I went in.

I found them all gathered in a large room with guns pointed at two men sitting at a table playing cards. Harold was tied to a chair, with cuts and wounds on his face. Trapper rushed over to him as

Harold raised his head. He smiled. "I knew you'd find me," he said.

Trapper yelled for an EMS call and untied Harold's bindings. Deacon had his men take the two hoods out and went to Harold, who was still sitting.

"Are you well enough to talk?" he asked.

Harold looked up and said he was. "I'm hurt, but not out. Ask away."

"Did you see anyone here that you knew?"

"I saw a man who had approached me last week about buying my property. He was a lawyer named Docktor."

Deacon looked up and smiled. "We got another one."

"Did Docktor say anything to you?"

"He said he knew I had lots of money and wanted to know where I kept it. They worked me over, I'm not a strong person, I gave in. I think they expected me to say it was in a bank, but I told them where to find it. They were surprised."

"That means Docktor was here, so Steve lied to us about not knowing him personally," Deacon said.

"Can I go home now, I'm getting tired of all this commotion, being arrested and then kidnapped. Then kidnapped again. I want it to all stop. I'm going to sell the property so people will stop bothering me." He looked like he was going to cry. Trapper helped him up and took him out of the room. Penny was standing at the entrance and Harold saw her. "Oh look, an angel."

I laughed and Penny gave me a look, I stopped. "Are you my angel?" Harold asked.

"If you'd like me to be," she replied and took his hand as the EMS unit roared in. They took Harold to it and the med techs checked him over and then they put him in the unit. Penny told Harold she'd be waiting for him. Trapper said he was going along and got in.

I turned to Deacon and said, "Now you have someone else to arrest."

"Yep, we got Docktor for conspiracy to murder, kidnapping and being a two timing shyster. I'm sure Ben Westeen will be happy to hear this."

All of Deacon's men left and we headed back to the precinct. I was trying to organize the whole thing in my head, but I got confused. Too many players in the case. Penny was quiet on the way back, she looked sleepy. Well, it was very early in the morning when this mess started. She was really good at helping to stop the criminals in the attic. I was very glad she could handle herself in those situations. I'd have to get her something really special for Christmas.

We arrived and Deacon came over to the car, I rolled down the window. "I'm having Docktor arrested as soon as I talk to the D.A. I can't wait to hear what he has to say. I'm sure we have enough on him with Harold's testimony to put him away for a long while. I'll need the two of you to make your statements also, about the incident in the attic. Why don't you two go get a rest, it's been a long morning and there's nothing to do now."

"Let me know when you pull Docktor in. I'd like to see what happens," I said.

"I'll call if anything develops. If you see Lynn at your office, tell her I'm sorry for rushing out of the house this morning."

"It's Saturday, the office is closed, so you will have to apologize yourself." He made a face and left us, I drove out. I looked to Penny and said, "Shall we go back home and cuddle?"

She just laughed.

*

Chapter 18

"I imagine Willy is highly perturbed with us. We may need to take him to play with Henry," I said.

"Fred is doing a good job around the building, I would say, with his flower gardens, and the lawn looking better than I've seen it in years," Penny replied. "Lacey told me the offices were being spotlessly cleaned."

"Yep, yesterday I suggested he get Buck to help him build a dog run for our animals. I'm sure they already have it just about finished. Let's get Willy and go see Fred and Henry." We went to the house and picked up Willy then drove to the office. I pulled into the back and was surprised to see Buck, Earl and Lynn on the side working on a fence with Fred. I had to laugh.

"About time you got here," Lynn said as we approached. I put Willy down and he went straight for Henry.

"How long have you been here and why?" I asked.

"Well, let's see. Buck is here because Fred talked him into building the dog run. I came because I had some reports to finish, and Earl came here to get away from Paula babysitting PJ at his apartment. We all got talked into working to get the fence poles cemented and the fencing put up. Fred can be pretty persuasive."

"Very nice," I said as I surveyed the nearly finished enclosure. "Penny and I just spent the morning catching criminals and finding huge amounts of cash. But I think you guys got more accomplished."

"Is this your Santa case?" Earl asked.

"Yes, how'd you know?"

"Fred mentioned it. He's still waiting for Angelo to call about the hitman."

I looked at Fred, he just shrugged his shoulders and said, "Nothing yet."

I went to Buck and asked him to go pull out the grill we bought last year and never used. He gave his trademark smile and went into the building.

"Grill? Don't you need food for that?" Lynn asked.

"Since you brought it up, you and Penny can run over to Tropicana and get some grillers and a couple side dishes," I said as I pulled out some money, handing it to her. "Don't forget refreshments."

"I know, beer and soda pop." She smiled and got her keys from her coat and took Penny to her car. They drove out and I went to help Buck pull the grill through the door.

An hour later, we had our food cooked and eaten. Then we all pitched in and finished the fencing. We put the gate on the back of it, then Fred and I took the dogs off the ropes and put them in the enclosure. They took to it right away, running back and forth down the twenty foot stretch that was six feet wide.

We cleaned up the picnic mess and the tools from building the fence and put everything away. Earl came to me, "Jim, you need any help on the Santa case? I'm open right now."

"Deacon has it pretty much sewn up for suspects. He just needs to put the pieces together and try to get a confession from the guiltiest person. But if we need help finding the hitman, I'll let you know."

"Good, I need to go in and make my report for a case I just finished, before Lacey tracks me down."

Lynn heard him and said, "I was going to do that before I got into construction. We can finish our reports, go rescue Paula and I'll get my baby. Then you can relax at home."

Earl grinned and they went into the building. I was standing, looking at the back of the building when Penny came up. "What's on your devious mind?" she asked.

"I think we need a picnic table back here." Buck was nearby and heard me.

"I'll take Fred and we'll go get one of those metal picnic tables that you put together," he said, I agreed and said to get a big one. I gave him the company credit card.

The dogs were still running around in the dog run, Fred had put a lock on the gate and gave me the keys to it. I said I would hang them on the wall next to the back door after putting them on a chain. I yelled to Buck to see if they could get a dog house for inside the run. He said they would look, and the two men took the van and left.

Penny kissed me and said, "You're going to turn the back of the building into an amusement park, aren't you?"

"That's not a bad idea. Maybe one of those bouncy castles and a water slide. I can get one of those big gazebo tents to shade us."

Penny just shook her head and went into the building.

~~*~~

"I did what you told me to do. I want the other half of my pay now," the man said to a bald man sitting at a desk. "Collisi is dead and the other Santa took the fall. Not my fault those P.I.s managed to get him off. They still don't know anything about me or you."

"Look, Dodge, I always cover myself and let others take blame for my actions. You, on the other hand, are the only person who knows who I am and about my involvement in this."

"Hey, I'm a pro. I do the job and move on to the next hit. I don't give a rat's ass about you or your involvement. I just want my pay and I'll be gone."

Santa Murders

The bald man stood and came around the desk. He took Dodge's arm and pulled him to a door. "Go in there, my assistant will give you your pay. And you get out of town, for your own good."

The hitman opened the door and went through, closing the door behind him. The bald man stood at the door and waited until he heard the gunshot, then it went quiet. The door opened and the man's assistant came in.

"What do you want me to do with him?"

The bald man said, "Put him and the Santa suit in his car and drive him out to the desert. Set him up in the driver's seat, then call the police and give them a tip. Make sure you put a few of Ben Westeen's business cards in his pocket. Just to add to the mystery. Don't leave any fingerprints either," the bald man said as his assistant was leaving.

"You got it boss, I'll take care of it."

~~*~~

I went to my office and sat, wondering what to do. I called Deacon to see if they found Docktor yet.

"My men can't locate him. No one seems to know where he is. One of his people said they think he went to his cottage out by Lake Mead. If he was supposed to be taking care of the divorce for Ben Westeen, I would think he'd hang around."

"Well, if Westeen did leave the country, maybe the lawyer went with him," I said.

"True, time will tell. I got a BOLO out for him. We'll find him in time," he said. He excused himself and took another call as I waited. He came back on and said, "Want to hear something interesting? Seems we got a tip about forty minutes ago regarding a dead man in a car. A patrol car went to check it out and found the man with a Santa suit and a 9mm handgun. The same caliber that murdered Collisi. Driver's license said his name was Hugo Dodge, and we have him in the records as being picked up on suspicion of murder in the past. Never convicted. Someone didn't want him to talk. Hold on." He went away again, then after a couple seconds, he came back.

"Listen to this, he had Ben Westeen's business cards on him. Looks like we have our hitman."

*

Chapter 19

"You know those business cards could have been planted," I said.

"Jim, you're too analytical. Let's just say this is the hitman. After ballistics confirms the gun was used to shoot Collisi, it's a lock."

""I'm sorry, I'm not trying to rain on your parade. I just look at things and want facts. I'll call Angelo and see what he knows about this guy."

"That works for me. Let me know what you find out. I have to go collect the crime scene. I hate going out to the desert." He hung up and I called Angelo. After a couple rings, he came on.

"Mr. R, what can I do for you?" he said with his distinctive voice.

"Angelo, do you know a Hugo Dodge?"

He was quiet for a moment, I let him think. "Hell yeah, I know the mook. Bad man. I hope you aren't going after him."

"Not anymore, he's been iced. They found him dead in his car out in the desert. Is he a hitman? And, could he be the fake Santa we were looking for?"

"I haven't gotten any confirmation on any hitmen hired out here, but I'd say he was a good bet for the crime."

"That's what I hoped to hear, my friend. How is the restaurant doing?"

"I'm trying to keep up with it. I can't believe the number of people wanting to get in to eat. I don't know who told all of them, but business is booming and I'm starting to turn people away."

"I'm happy for your success. I'll let you go, I have to call Deacon with the info you gave me."

"No problem, Mr. R, it's good that Dodge isn't in your sights."

"Appreciate the warning, and thanks for the extra men yesterday, they were helpful. We'll talk later," I said and hung up.

I sat back in my chair for a while, thinking. This hitman meets his demise in the desert. Sounds like a mob hit. And why pin Ben Westeen with this? He wanted Collisi's help to buy the property. Why kill him? Something wasn't right.

I went out to the hallway, and looking through the glass doors to the front, I saw Penny at Lacey's desk on her phone. I heard a noise from the back and turned to see Buck come in with Fred. He saw me and said they were getting tools to put the picnic table together.

"Did you find a dog house?" I asked.

"Sure did, a nice big one that will get both dogs out of the weather," he replied. They took the tools out. I jumped when I turned to find Penny standing behind me. Her ninja-like talents baffled me.

"What are you up to?" I asked her.

"Gordy called me about doing a Christmas special and asked if I knew a Santa. I told him I'd talk to you."

"Well, you know I do know Santa personally. I'll ask him."

"Good, have him call me and I'll arrange it with Gordy." She turned and went back to the lobby as silently as she came. She amazed me.

I went back to my office and sat. I pulled out my cell phone and speed dialed Deacon to give him Angelo's take on the hitman. He sounded like he was far away and he didn't sound happy at all.

"Where are you?" I asked.

"Where did I tell you I was going?" he said snippily. "I'm in the desert, and not pleased. Dodge was shot with a bullet to the head from the front, and Joe Lang doesn't think he was murdered in the car. No blood spatter. This is not the crime scene. He was planted here for our benefit. So who ever hired him did the deed, that lets Lila off the hook. Unless she hired another hitman. I don't think her husband would give her any more money to do that. Now the lawyer may have whacked him, or had him done in. We're still looking for him and Westeen. Warren said he can't find any record of Westeen going out of the country. So I have a BOLO out on both men."

"Maybe a trip to Westeen's office would do some good?" I said.

"I was thinking that, shake up a few employees and see what pops up. I need to get out of this hell hole. I wish they never built Vegas in the desert."

"Well, when it was first settled it was a meadow with trees and water. Las Vegas means 'The Meadow' and after years of developing, it became cement and high rises."

"Thank you for the history lesson, I'll meet you at Westeen's. As soon as I find out where it is." He hung up.

I went to my computer and pulled up Google. I did a search on Westeen and found the location of his office. I'd call Deacon when I got there to be sure we were at the same place. I went out and found Penny talking to Buck and Fred.

"I have to go chase bad guys, you want to go?" I asked her.

"I've had enough. I'm going to stay here and play with Willy and Henry while the men finish the picnic table. Lynn said she'd give me a ride home when she finished her reports. Besides, I want to see Paula and little PJ."

"Okay, I'll see you later then," I said, kissed her, and went to my car.

I drove over to the location of Westeen's office and saw Deacon standing in the parking lot. Good, I wouldn't have to track him down. I saw Warren was with him as I parked.

"Anything new since I last talked to you?" I asked as I approached them.

"Nope, we just got here. Shall we shake some trees and see if Westeen falls out?" Deacon smiled and went to the entrance.

"You know it's Saturday, the building may be closed," I said.

"You're just a ray of sunshine today, aren't you?" he replied.

I was laughing to myself, but I was feeling that Deacon was getting a little crabby lately. I enjoy cracking jokes, but he seemed a little uptight. I wondered if it was the job, or the baby, or Lynn working with us and not at the precinct. Either way, I would have to subtly talk to him about it.

We got to the door and went in. There was a security guard at the front counter and he smiled at us. "What can I do for you today, officers?"

"It's detectives, and how did you know?"

"Name's Ralph Samuels, I used to be with North Vegas Police." He held out a hand to Deacon. "I retired and can still spot a cop, even in civies," he said with a smile.

"Glad for you, Ralph. I need to know the location of Ben Westeen. I know he's not out of the country like we were told earlier. You wouldn't have an ear to the door about his whereabouts?" Deacon asked.

Ralph leaned on the counter and smiled. "I'm sworn to secrecy, but I could care less about Westeen. He's a miserable man, and I'd like to see him get his due." He looked around the lobby and then said, "I hear scuttlebutt about him being with his girlfriend while his wife cools her heels in jail. They are supposed to be out at Lake Mead in his lawyer's cabin. Of course, you didn't hear that from me."

"Of course, I don't even know you. When did he go?"

"I guess they went out there late last night. He was here until midnight and then left with his lady friend. I did hear him asking her if she had her bathing suit packed."

"Good to know, Ralph. You wouldn't by chance know where his lawyer, Ben Docktor, is?"

"That S.O.B. is here in the building now. He got here about a half hour ago and went up to Westeen's floor. I presume he's in Westeen's office."

Deacon turned to Warren and told him to call for fast back-up. "What floor is he on?" he asked Ralph.

"Sixth," he replied.

Deacon looked happy and said, "We got Harold's kidnapper."

*

Chapter 20

Five minutes later, the closest patrol cars to the building roared up and the officers rushed to the entrance.

Ralph said, "I love to see a good team of men storming the castle."

Deacon smiled and replied, "We have good men."

The officers entered and went to Deacon. "We have a suspect on the sixth floor that is wanted for kidnaping and conspiracy to murder. Take care, I want him alive, but anything changes, go with your instincts. Let's go."

They went to the elevators and filled the small cab. It rose up towards the sixth floor and before the doors opened, Deacon said, "Be alert, I don't think he knows we are coming. But be observant."

They nodded, and I could feel the tension in the small compartment. As the elevator stopped at the designated floor, everyone backed against the walls and waited to see what would happen when the doors opened.

We watched the doors slide back and Deacon looked out, saying, "It's clear."

All the officers poured into the hallway. Deacon had asked Ralph for directions to Westeen's office, so he knew where to turn. He led us to a door, he tried it, but it was locked. There was a frosted glass panel beside the door and Deacon could see someone moving in the room. He couldn't make out who it was, but he knew Docktor was the only one in the building. He stood back and rushed the door. It blew open and everyone streamed in.

There was an older woman, who looked shocked, as she was surrounded by cops with guns. "What the hell?" she said.

Deacon went to her and said, "Who are you?"

"Betsy, I clean these offices. Who are you?"

Deacon looked embarrassed and said, "Police, ma'am. Do you know Ben Docktor?"

"Yes, I do. He was here, but left rather quickly. I don't know where he went."

Deacon turned to his men and said, "Search the floor. He has to be here somewhere. Harris," he ordered to one man, "watch the elevator. Make sure no one gets on it."

Harris went off as Deacon turned back to me. "I don't know the layout of this floor, maybe there's a stairway going down. How did he know we were here?"

I looked to Westeen's desk and found the answer to Deacon's question. A monitor showed a view from the security cameras in the lobby. I pointed towards the screen, "He saw us coming. He knew we were here."

"He had to figure we were after him. He's on the run now. Damn."

We heard a couple gunshots from the hallway and hustled towards the door. Deacon peeked around the doorframe and then went out. We saw two patrolmen kneeling with their weapons aimed at another office door. They fired again and shots were returned. They moved away as we went to join the shootout. Deacon inched to the door and peeked again. One shot hit where his head had been just seconds ago.

"Damn, that was close." Deacon saw one of the officers move to a door down the hall and go in. Deacon peeked in again and was greeted with another gunshot.

"Docktor, we have all day out here. I sent for more back-up and you can't get off this floor without going through us. So why don't you just give up." Deacon gave Warren a silent signal to make a call. Warren went down the hall to call for help.

There was no sound from the room as we waited. Deacon said, "Docktor, this is futile. Give it up and live."

We could hear a small voice say, "Screw you."

Deacon looked to me, "He sounds weak, like maybe we hit him. I don't want him dying on my watch. Too much we need to know."

He peeked in the door again, this time with no gunfire. He looked further and saw a man on the floor bleeding. Deacon took the chance and turned into the room with his gun out in front. The man on the floor made no effort to move. Deacon yelled for Warren to get an EMS unit.

I followed Deacon into the room and could see that Docktor was passed out on the floor. I went up next to Deacon and stood looking down at the man. Suddenly, Docktor raised his gun and I pushed Deacon out of the way as he fired. Deacon returned fire and hit the man in the chest.

I'm not a med tech, but I could tell he was dead. Deacon yelled for Warren to cancel the bus and call Joe Lang.

We stood looking down at the man's lifeless body. "Damn it! I wanted him alive. Why couldn't I have missed, like I usually do?"

I cracked a smile. He looked to me and said, "Don't you start laughing, I don't want to start. This isn't funny." He looked away as his men came into the room. Deacon told them, "Secure the scene and wait for the ME and CSI. I need to go down to the lobby and let Ralph know."

He turned and went out, I followed. In the elevator I said, "You still have a case, with or without Docktor."

"I know, but I would have liked to fry a shyster." He smiled.

We got to the lobby and Ralph was in a panic. "I wanted to call you, but didn't know how to reach you. Docktor just left the building."

"What!" Deacon shouted.

"After you went up, he came down the stairs and went out the side door. I debated whether to go up, but you came down."

Deacon looked frustrated, but said, "I have a second chance at the bastard."

Deacon turned to Ralph and said, "Who was with him going up?"

"He was alone. I didn't see anyone else," Ralph said.

"Well, there was another man who was shooting at us. Hold on." He placed another call and said, "Warren, take a photo of the dead man." He waited and then the photo came up on his phone. He turned it to Ralph, "Does this man look familiar?"

Ralph looked closely and said, "Yeah, he's one of Docktor's assistants. Don't know him personally, but I've seen him with Docktor."

"Thanks Ralph. If you see Docktor again, call me," he said, handing the man his card.

"I will, and I'll call if Westeen comes back, too."

"Excellent. Now I have to clean up this mess." He turned away and pulled his cell phone. He was calling for another BOLO on Docktor.

Back in the elevator I asked, "What are you going to do about Lila?"

"I wish I knew, she committed some crimes and will go down for those. In light of everything, I don't think that she had anything to do with Collisi's murder. So I'll have to revise the charges."

"That should make her happy, I'm sure."

"I couldn't care less. I want the main person who set this whole thing in motion. I want who hired the hitman to kill Collisi, then framed your friend, and got Lila involved along with Ben Westeen. I think Ben Docktor is a different part of this case. I think Westeen told Docktor about Harold's money and he went after it, kidnapping Harold."

"I have every faith in you to wrap this up," I said.

Deacon smiled and said, "You're just being nice to me so I don't arrest you and Trapper for obstruction of justice."

"That would be nice." I smiled.

*

Chapter 21

We stepped off the elevator and went back to the room where Docktor's assistant was bleeding on the plush beige carpeting. Deacon stood looking down at the man lying face up. "I didn't have time to get a good look at Docktor when he was with Westeen in observation. I wouldn't know this man from another by his face. I need to see a picture of Docktor so I'll know him next time I see him." He called to Warren. "See if you can find a photo of Docktor, please."

Warren went off and we waited for the ME, Joe Lang, to arrive. "You know I like to relax on Saturdays after having my hands inside people's guts all week," he said with a flourish as he entered the room. "I always wanted to see inside this building. Offices of the famous entrepreneur, Benjamin Westeen. Not as gaudy as I figured. Now what do we have here?"

He bent down and studied the dead man, examining the wounds and checking his eyes. "Yep, I rule that he's dead. Who shot him?"

Deacon didn't say anything, so I said, "Deacon and his dead-eye. Just after I saved his life by pushing him out of the line of fire."

"I suppose you're not going to let me forget that?" Deacon said quietly. I just snickered.

"Well, it was a clean shot. No crime to solve here. Death posted at…" he looked at his watch, then shook his wrist. "Damn watch stopped. Anyone know what time it is?"

Deacon answered, "2:45 PM. Give or take a couple minutes."

"Thanks, I'll note it in my report, give or take a couple minutes." Joe stood and called for his men to come in and bag the body. "I presume you have identified the body?"

Deacon said, "No, I haven't."

Joe proceeded to check the pockets of the man's clothes and handed the contents to Deacon who put on gloves and pulled an evidence bag. Deacon opened the wallet and said, "Name's Marcus Rawlings of Los Angeles. I wonder what he was doing here?"

He turned to Warren who re-entered the room with a photo of Docktor, Deacon asked him to run the guy. Warren pulled some kind of tablet from his pocket and did some typing. I had seen those tablets on shows like NCIS, where you could get information on criminals. I didn't know LVPD had them.

"New toy?" I asked Warren as I looked over his shoulder at the screen, now bringing up a photo of Rawlings.

"Just got them last week, they are so cool. I'm connected to about six different crime databases and Google," Warren said.

I watched as more information showed up. Warren looked up and told Deacon, "This guy was wanted in California for fleeing a murder charge. I guess I should tell LAPD that we got him."

"Isn't there a form on that thing to report back to LA?" I asked.

"No, have to call the old fashion way, by phone," Warren said with a smile and pulled his cell phone. Deacon was studying the photo, which I assumed Warren had gotten from the LEIN computer in their car.

"So, you did good, shooting him," I said to Deacon. "Another bad guy off the streets."

"Still doesn't make it any easier killing a man." Deacon wasn't smiling, he looked serious.

"Let's get out of here and go to the offices of Docktor, maybe we'll find him there. Greg, take charge here until the scene has been cleared."

Warren agreed and Deacon and I went to the elevator again. On the way down we were silent. The car stopped at the lobby and we exited. I stopped Deacon in the lobby and said I wanted to talk.

"I don't want to pry, but I've known you for a number of years now. We've been through a lot of crimes and danger together, so I get concerned when I see you acting strange. You've been a bit cranky lately and I'm worried."

Deacon smiled slightly. He went to the easy chairs in the lobby and sat. I sat across from him and wondered what he was doing.

He sat back and sighed. "Jim, I've been through a lot of changes since I first met you and Penny. My life was simpler back then. I was just a cop doing my job. Then I hurt myself when I took that bullet for Penny. That was a big deal to me. Both saving her life and having my hip replaced to repair the damage. Then we came out here to Vegas where I met Lynn and ended up staying. All the changes in my work here, from being a low grade detective to Sergeant, and then with Lynn leaving the force, I moved to Lieutenant and took her job. I was a simple cop, now I have more responsibilities that sometimes overwhelm me. Having the baby and the lack of sleep that goes with it don't help. I love my wife and baby, and I love my job, but sometimes I feel like running off and hiding."

I didn't know what to say. I waited, then had to say something. "Deacon, I care for you, you're a great friend and I respect you for what you've accomplished in such a short time. My life has turned around so much since I was just a simple guy sitting in a bedroom minding my own business. The classmate murders started both of us on a journey that I hope never ends. I understand your feelings, I've been there too. I'll always be here to help get you through the tough times. Just don't be afraid to talk to me, don't hold it in. Now, shall we go nab Docktor?"

Deacon smiled and stood. "I think that would make me feel better." We left the lobby and went to our cars. I told Deacon I'd follow him.

~~*~~

"I'm not happy about the mess this is turning into. Westeen is off playing footsie with his concubine and Docktor is on the run. Stupid people," the bald man said into the phone. "Lila Westeen is useless and I need to have this problem with the property on Industrial solved soon. I need that property and I can't keep getting others involved. They will screw up the deal. Take care of both

Westeen and Docktor and report back to me." He hung up the phone and turned to the man standing at his desk.

The man said, "If we keep murdering people, this will get messy. Collisi was no big deal, but to murder Westeen and his lawyer will take the focus off them for what you want to do. The cops will start looking elsewhere. Right now, the cops will waste so much time and energy on Westeen and Docktor they won't come after us."

The bald man sat thinking. "I didn't want this to turn into a circus. Which it has. Okay, call Fremlin back and cancel the hits. I need to go at this from a different tact. That preacher won't sell, we have to convince him to do so. Forcing the man won't help, we need to get to him from a different direction. Call Yvonne and have her see me. Maybe we can seduce him into selling."

"But Lila tried that and it didn't work."

"That was because Lila was married, so she couldn't offer Renford what he wanted—a wife."

*

Chapter 22

"What makes you think Renford needs a wife?"

"He probably doesn't, but Yvonne has a way of luring men to marry her. She's worked well for me in the past and left a string of dead husbands. This is Vegas and people get married all the time in an instant. All she has to do is get him to say 'I do' and we got him. He can have a terrible accident that is seen by many witnesses and Yvonne is a rich widow."

"Why couldn't Yvonne take the millions she'll get from his death and tell you to go to hell?"

"Because I have something on her that she values more than screwing me over. I'm not worried about it. Just call her and get her in here today. And call off the hits."

"Okay, it's your show. I'll call." He went out of the room and the bald man sat back looking at the mock-up model of the casino/hotel he planned to build on Renford's property. He had enough cash to buy the property, but Renford was holding out. Not a smart move, but the bald man had to be careful not to lose the deal with Renford. Yvonne will get the job done. He smiled and lit up the Cuban cigar he was rolling around in his mouth for the last half hour.

~~*~~

Deacon and I went to Docktor's office and found it locked up. Deacon said, "I didn't figure we'd find him here. Since he assumes we are after him, he'll be out of circulation. He may even leave the city. I'm sure by now he knows we have his men in custody, and that they talked. I'd say he will be hanging a sign on this door that says 'out of business.'"

I was pressing my face to the window next to the door and trying to see inside. It was a typical office—lobby, reception desk, waiting room with furniture and a hallway going to who knows where. I didn't know, but I could see shadows moving on the wall in a room down the hall. I told Deacon. He looked into the window and then started to bang on the door while still looking in the window. The shadows stopped moving, then the light in the room shut off.

Deacon reared up his leg and applied it to the door. It flew open and we rushed in. I whispered to Deacon, "You have probable cause?"

Santa Murders

"Locked door, office closed up, dark shadows moving in a room, I'd say there was a robbery going on. My probable cause," he said with a big grin.

We went down the hallway to the room in question and carefully went to the door. There was a loud noise, like a chair that tipped over. Deacon rushed the room with his gun out front and yelled to stop. I couldn't see who he was yelling at, but came up behind Deacon. Then I saw him.

The man was trying to climb out one of those half windows that opened sideways, but wasn't quite wide enough for a human to squeeze through. The man was caught and couldn't move. I had to laugh as he struggled to get through. His belt was caught on the handle, and he hadn't noticed.

Deacon went over and grabbed him, pulling the man back through the window. He fell to the ground and I turned on the room lights. Deacon stared at the man and said, "Damn, it's not Docktor."

Deacon pointed his weapon at the man's head and yelled, "Talk, and quickly, I'm in a bad mood today. My trigger finger may slip. What are you doing here?"

Deacon actually frightened me. The man was shaking on the floor and said, "I was told to come here and get certain files. That's all, don't shoot."

"Who told you?"

"Docktor, he called me and said to break into the office and take out certain files. I have a list and was starting to work on it when you busted in."

Deacon looked to me and said, "I told you it was a robbery."

Deacon pulled the man up from the floor and pushed him into a chair. "Okay, where's this list?"

"It's in my head. I have a really good memory and don't have to write things down."

Deacon went to the desk and picked up a pad of paper and a pen. He tossed them at the man and said, "Write down everything and don't leave anything out. My mood hasn't changed."

The man nodded quickly and started to write. We stood, watching him write, and then he finished. He handed the pad to Deacon and he looked it over. He handed it to me and I looked at it. I saw about five files that had no significance to me. They were all listed as case file numbers for criminal court and they were in order of dates. I turned to the file cabinet and opened one that had the same number group as the first file listed. I pulled the folder from the file cabinet and opened it.

Santa Murders

"I think you should look at this," I said to Deacon. He came over and I pointed to something in the file. He smiled and pulled his cell phone. He was talking to Warren and told him to come to Docktor's office. Deacon handcuffed the man to a chair and we waited.

Ten minutes later, Warren came in with a couple patrolmen. Deacon told the officers to take the man into a holding cell until he could get back to the precinct. "Greg, take this list and pull the rest of the files from these cabinets and bring them in. I have someplace to go."

Deacon and I left the offices and went back to our cars. I asked where we were going. Deacon smiled and said, "We're taking a little trip. Follow me."

I knew that the file I gave him was a case file for a B&E on a cabin at Lake Mead. The perp who was nabbed at the scene was a young man named Joel Harris. I thought that name sounded familiar, it was Harold's assistant at the church. Deacon and I got his name when we were at the church and wanted to go upstairs. Deacon asked him his name before we went up. I wondered if Harold knew he had a criminal working for him.

We drove out and over to Industrial Road and into the church parking lot. We got out and went in. The two bruisers Angelo sent were in the middle of the room watching everyone moving around. They saw us come in and came over.

"Has Harold had any problems?" I asked.

The one hulk said, "All is quiet."

Harold saw us and came over. "Hey guys, what's up?"

Deacon asked, "Where's your assistant Joel?"

"Joel? He's in the back getting more decorations."

"Take us to him," Deacon asked. Harold led us to the back where we found Joel coming out with boxes of bulbs for the tree. He suddenly looked surprised, but he was too close to run from us.

Deacon asked the boy if he knew Ben Docktor. The young man looked really spooked now.

"I said I wouldn't tell anyone about the video. I told Docktor that."

*

Chapter 23

"What videos?" Deacon asked, once we had Joel sitting in a chair in Harold's office.

"Last year, I broke into Docktor's cabin at Lake Mead and I found that he liked to video tape his love interests. I took a couple of the videos and played them on the recorder in his cabin. I knew some of the women in the videos, one was Lila Westeen. I got caught by neighborhood security while I was watching them. Docktor said he'd get me off if I kept quiet about what I saw and worked for him. I never told him that I saw him with Lila. I knew he was Ben Westeen's lawyer and it might cause a problem."

"You're lucky you aren't dead. How did you end up working for Harold?" Deacon asked.

"Docktor wanted someone inside the church. He said it was because Westeen wanted to buy Harold's property. I was spying and reporting back to Docktor. I came to the church offering my services and Harold hired me."

"Did you know Harold had money stashed away?"

"No, not until Docktor told me what Ben Westeen had heard during the police questioning. I was going to look myself, but police came here before I could find it. By then, Docktor had grabbed Harold and found out where the money was. I just kept silent when they got here to take the money."

"Did the men who came to take the money know you?"

"I never saw those men before that day. I just went along with it and kept quiet."

Deacon stood and took me out of the room. "So, Joel was put here to spy on Harold. Docktor had the wheels in motion before Lila even hit on Harold. That tells me Ben Westeen didn't know what was going on. It may clear him."

"But, who was Docktor working for to get the property? As a lawyer, he couldn't do much with the property. He had to be working for someone and then he found out about the hidden money and got greedy."

"I guess we need Docktor to find that out, and if we had him, I doubt he would talk." We didn't have anything on Joel to arrest him. Deacon told

Harold he should think about whether he should keep Joel working for him or not.

Harold told us, "I like Joel, and he does good work. If he promises to keep his mouth shut about my life, I'll keep him around."

Deacon looked to Joel, "You got a second chance, don't blow it. I'll be watching you."

Joel nodded his head and said he'd be good. Deacon told him he may have to testify if needed. Joel agreed.

We left the building and I asked Deacon where he was off to next.

He looked at his watch and said, "I haven't seen my wife and baby in over a day. I'm calling it quits and going home. You should too. I'll talk to you tomorrow." He went to his car and I went to mine. I watched him drive out and I followed.

~~*~~

The woman came to Harold's door about an hour after he was alone in his office. Joel said he'd continue decorating and went back out.

"Excuse me, are you Harold?" she asked.

Harold jumped to his feet seeing the very attractive redhead standing there. "I am. What can I do for you?"

"I don't want to interrupt, but I wanted to meet with you. I heard so much about you, I was intrigued. I'm sorry, I'm Yvonne Wahl. No relation to the hair clipper people," she said with a laugh.

Harold was struck by her beauty, but most of all by her voice. So light and lilting, airy and almost like a nightingale singing. If he ever heard a nightingale. He moved around the desk and said, "May I help you?"

"Please, don't fuss over me. I just wanted to meet you. I hear you do so much for the poor and indigent around Vegas, I admire you so much. You are a saint among the sinners here in this heathen town."

Harold pulled a chair over for her, she thanked him and sat. "I'm happy you feel that way about what I do. Most people don't care about helping the poor. Are you a patron of our shelters and soup kitchens?"

"No, that's what I wanted to ask. If you could help me to help others. I have a good deal of money and don't know where to use it to help people."

Santa Murders

Harold grinned widely at having found a woman as well off as he was, and she wanted to help the poor. She was smiling back at him. She hoped he was going down.

~~*~~

My cell phone buzzed early the next morning. It was Sunday and after eight, so I wasn't annoyed. The caller ID said private, but I gave up ignoring those long ago. Usually, they were a client wanting to be anonymous. I answered and it was Joel from the church. I had given him my card and told him to call me if anything happened to Harold. I started to worry.

"Joel, what's up?" I replied when he told me who he was.

"Mr. Richards, you told me to call you if anything was going on. Well, I think you need to come here."

"What is it?"

"I think it would be better if you came here," he said again.

"Do I need to rush? Where are Harold's bodyguards?"

"I'd say it would be a good idea to come soon. The men are still here, but Harold is missing again."

I perked up on that. "Okay, I have to make a call and then I'll be there." I hung up and called Trapper.

"Harold's missing," I said when he answered.

"What? Where, how?" He sounded half awake.

"Harold's assistant called me and said he was missing. I'm going there now, can you meet me?"

"I'm getting dressed now, later." He hung up and I pulled my clothes on. Penny was in the kitchen and saw me come out.

"What's up?"

"Harold is missing again. I'm going to meet Trapper at the church."

"I'll get my bag and gather Willy," she said and went off.

I yelled to hurry up. She was ready in two minutes and heading out the door. I had to keep up with her. We took my car and drove to the church.

161

Santa Murders

Trapper was already there and we went in the building. Joel was standing in the middle of the well decorated room. He ran to us.

"I don't see anything that suggests he was taken," the young man said.

"Where are the bodyguards?" Trapper asked.

"They're outside looking around the building for signs of forced entry. I was here all night putting up decorations, and then I fell asleep on the couch over there. Harold and the lady were still in his office at that time."

"Lady? What lady?" I asked.

"I don't know who she was, but Harold and she spent a lot of time in his office. I waited, but got too tired."

Trapper and I looked to each other. I wasn't happy hearing some new woman entered his life right now.

The doors to the front flew open and in came Harold with a woman in a short white dress. He smiled to us and announced, "Congratulate us, we got married!"

*

Chapter 24

I stood in place, shocked at the announcement. Trapper sprang into action and went to Harold, taking him by the arm and pulling him away from the woman. I went to them.

"What the hell are you talking about?" Trapper demanded.

The woman came over and said, "Excuse me, but Harold is my husband now and I have every right to be by his side."

"Well, you can go stand by someone else's side. I've known this man for over thirty years and I want to talk to him, without you. So move along."

Harold looked confused. "I don't have anything to hide from Yvonne. We are soul partners and I can share whatever I say with her."

"Fine Harold, but I want to talk to you one on one, man to man, friend to friend. Without a person, who I don't know, listening to what I have to say."

Harold turned to the woman and said, "Yvonne, why don't you go to my office, there is champagne in the tall cabinet I was saving for a special occasion."

The woman was glaring at Trapper, but left us. She went to the office and Trapper pulled Harold off to the side.

"What were you thinking?"

"She's wonderful, I was so taken by her. I knew it was love. Soul mates. She's perfect for me. She has money like I do, and she cares for the poor. We talked all night, then we just couldn't wait. We found a chapel open on the strip and got married. This is a first for me."

"Yea, well I hope it's not the last," Trapper said.

"What are you talking about? She's perfect for me," he said again.

"Harold, you don't know this woman. What's her background, her family, does she have a criminal past?"

"I don't care, we talked and she told me things I wanted to hear from a woman."

"Of course, Harold. She knows what to say. She wanted to marry you. For your money."

"Oh, no. She has money like I do."

"Have you seen a bank book with all this money?"

"I don't believe she would lie to me. I'm happy and that's all that counts."

Trapper paused then said, "May I see the marriage license?"

Harold reached into his jacket and took it out, handing it to Trapper. He opened the paper and read the certificate. "Yvonne Wahl? That's her name? Did she show proof to the chapel?"

"Of course, they are careful who they marry."

Trapper let Harold go and stood back. "You are nuts. You are blind and nuts. She will take all your money, and if you think about it, she owns half of all your property now. Think about that."

"I'm not worrying about it," Harold replied.

"Fine, think about this. If you die, she gets it all. I hope you watch your back."

"Will, you are worrying about nothing," he said as the woman was approaching us again.

Trapper turned to her and said, "If anything happens to Harold, I'm coming after you. Don't forget that." Then he turned and went to the front door. I just stood there waiting for my cue. Trapper finally turned and said, "Are you coming?"

I moved away from Harold and his new wife. I didn't like her from the minute I saw her, she seemed evil. I would talk to Deacon to see what he could come up with on her. I saw the two bruisers standing by the door and told them, "You keep a very close eye on Harold, or I'll have Angelo give you a serious talk if anything happens to him." They just nodded nervously and I went out.

In the parking lot, Trapper burst, "What the hell was he thinking! After his kidnappings and everyone trying to get his property, he marries a woman he doesn't know. She's after his money and property, simple as that! I've tried to help him, but if he wants to lose everything, I'm not going to stop him, if he doesn't care."

"You know you'll be there for him," I said.

"Yvonne Wahl. I need to get Deacon to run her down. She has to have a record. He'll come up with something, I'm sure of it.

I realized that Penny had followed me into the church. She wasn't with us now. I got panicky. "I have to find Penny," I said as I went back to the church. Penny was standing just inside the door.

"You forgot me," she said briskly. "But I forgive you, since you had a lot on your mind."

I looked around the room and Harold was not there. I presumed they went into his office to celebrate. "I'm sorry. Yes, I had things on my mind."

"After you and Trapper left, that horrible woman was saying bad things about the two of you to Harold. She didn't see me standing here."

"How can anyone miss you?" I asked.

"I was wondering that," she said with a grin. "She's definitely not a housewife. She finally looked at me and didn't recognize me. I was offended."

"She probably isn't from here if she didn't know you. I'm calling Deacon, if Trapper hasn't already, to see what he can find out about her. Let's get out of here, I've had enough of this place." We left and went back to our car.

Trapper was still in the parking lot in his car. He said from his window, "I'm going into the office, if you'd care to join me. I'm calling Deacon." He drove off and Penny and I got in our car. She was still holding Willy in his purse and he was resting quietly. I envied him.

We got back to the office and parked. Fred was in the back with Henry, taking him for a run. Willy shot after them when Penny put him down. Fred opened the gate to the new dog run and put Henry in. Willy followed him and Fred closed the gate.

Trapper said hello to Fred as he went into the building. Penny went to Fred to watch the dogs play. I excused myself and went in to Trapper's office.

I sat in his client chair while Trapper called Deacon. He put him on the speaker and Deacon said hello.

"Deacon, it's Will and Jim. Guess what? Harold got married this morning," Trapper said before Deacon could respond. "I want to ask you if you can run a background on the woman to see what she's up to." Trapper finally took a breath.

"Will, is Harold in danger?" Deacon said through the phone.

"He got married, what more do you need?" Trapper replied.

I tried not to laugh.

Deacon said. "Okay, I see problems with this. Who is this woman that he fell in love with and married?"

"According to the marriage license, her name is, or was, Yvonne Wahl. Can you check on her?"

"I'll see what I can do. You think she's after his money?"

"What do you think? I feel like I'm waiting for Harold to have a fatal accident in front of a city bus."

"I'll run the name and see what comes up, but it could be a fake name. Do you have a photo?"

Trapper had nothing to say. I spoke up, "I figured we'd need something to fall back on, so I recorded the whole thing on video."

Trapper stared at me and said, "I've said it before, you are creepy."

*

Chapter 25

"Jim, can you email me the video?" Deacon asked over the speaker.

"I can do that, hold on." I pressed a couple buttons on my cell phone and tapped the screen. I selected email and tapped on Deacon's address, then sent it. "You should get it shortly. It's a big file."

"Okay, I'll send it in to forensics and see if they can get facial recognition. Thanks. Is Harold in the church now?"

Trapper spoke, "That's where we left him."

"Alone?"

"No, Angelo's goons are still there," I said. "I don't think even this woman could chase them away."

"I hope they watch him carefully. Harold got kidnapped while they were watching him, now he gets married. Were they part of the wedding?"

"Again, they didn't see him go. I'll have to see if Angelo can put more men on him," I said.

Deacon said he'd get on the video and the background check. "This woman showing up suddenly could have something to do with the murder of Collisi and all the attempts on Harold. Maybe the person behind it all is sending in his last resort."

"Let us know what you find," Trapper said, and he disconnected the conversation. He looked to me and said, "I shouldn't be so involved with Harold. I hardly knew him all these years. But the guy grows on you. I just hate to see him get screwed." He stood and I followed him out of the room.

We went back outside where Penny and Fred were sitting on the new picnic table. It was probably the largest one they had, it could seat ten people easily. Fred went off to feed the dogs.

I sat and Penny asked, "Anything on the debbil?"

I gave her a strange look, then realized what she said. "No, the devil is still unknown. Deacon is going to check on her. All we can do now is wait." My phone buzzed and I looked at the caller ID, Joel was calling again, I put him on speaker. "What's up Joel, is Harold all right?"

"Harold's all right, he's mooning over this woman. I don't like her, she chased me out of his office so they could be alone. But that's not why I called." He paused, then continued when I didn't speak. "I got a call from Docktor and he wanted to know what I told you guys. He must be watching me. I told him I said nothing that you didn't already know. I'm afraid now. What should I do?"

Trapper looked at me and said to the phone, "Sit tight and I'll see you get protection. Just lay low for now and we'll come get you. And stay away from the she-devil." He smiled and I hung up.

"What are we going to do for him?" I asked.

"I'll call Deacon. If Joel is becoming our link to Docktor, we may need him alive." He stood and went back into the building.

Penny shifted back to me. "I invited Fred to our house tonight for dinner."

"I'm okay with that, where are you going to get the dinner? Send out or call my daughter?" She hit me, although I was expecting that.

"I'm inviting a few people from my studio and I wanted Fred to make up for the lack of men."

Lack of men, that didn't sound good. "Why are there a lack of men coming? Or should I say not coming."

"I mostly work with women that help me get ready for my job. I thought it would be nice to have them to the house for a dinner. There will be a number of women attending."

"You aren't trying to set Fred up are you?" I asked.

"Me? No, I just thought that maybe Fred would like to wear one of the nice outfits I helped him buy the other day while you were off fighting evil debbils."

She amazed me. I didn't know she took Fred out. Whatever, he looked happy.

Trapper came back out and said, "I talked to Deacon, he's going to meet us at the church, if you want to go?"

I looked at Penny. She said, "I'll take your car, you go with Will to your crime scene. I need to get the house ready for tonight."

I said that would be fine with me. I asked Trapper if I could hitch a ride, he said it was good. I stood, kissed Penny and followed Trapper.

Santa Murders

In the car on the way back to the church, Trapper asked, "So what does Penny have planned for you tonight?"

"A party for her female co-workers and Fred. I feel sorry for the guy. I think she's trying to set him up."

"Why not, Fred is a nice guy despite the fact he was once a mob figure. So was Angelo. I'm sure he's a real catch."

"I hope he doesn't get hurt. The women out here like to take on a man and then dump him."

"You're being too harsh on these women. They're no different than women from back in Michigan."

"That's why I worry. Well, he's been homeless for over ten years, so he may need some female companionship."

"I hope he remembers what to do." Trapper laughed.

"I'm sure Penny's women will remind him."

We pulled up to the building and saw Deacon's car in the parking lot. We figured he must have already been inside. Entering the building, we saw Harold talking to Deacon. Joel was with them.

The new wife was nowhere to be seen. We went to them.

"Harold, this is your church. You've been here for years, you are in charge, not this woman who you hardly know," Deacon was saying to Harold.

"I know, but I put her in charge of the church. It relieves me from worrying about the small details."

"Harold, Joel is no small detail. She shouldn't fire him without talking it over with you," Deacon said in an annoyed voice.

Joel looked upset, and Harold was acting like nothing was wrong. "Yvonne said she didn't trust Joel, since he was working for Docktor. She felt he had betrayed my trust. I think she was right."

Trapper moved forward, probably understanding the situation. "Harold, Joel was coerced into what he did. He didn't do it to hurt you. It is getting really scary watching this woman take over. Where is your head? Besides being wrapped up in her. Have you had sex with her yet?"

"Will! That's not something I wish to reveal to anyone. My relationship with Yvonne is spiritual. We live on another plane of life. Sex is not important."

Trapper turned to me and grinned. Deacon said, "Doesn't matter, Joel had a place to stay here. Your wife is throwing him out. He's being threatened by some bad guys, are you going to let him be homeless with them waiting around for him?"

Harold looked at the boy and said, "I don't want anything to happen to him. But my wife explained it all to me. It's better if he leaves and takes the danger with him. You're the police, you take care of him." He turned and walked away from us.

Trapper spoke, "Damn, that woman has him spellbound."

*

Chapter 26

"What about me?" Joel pleaded.

"I'll see you get protective custody. I think you should talk to the D.A. about your involvement with Docktor. We already have a warrant out for him, but you may add some fuel to the fire. Did he say where he was at when he called?"

"No, he said he wouldn't be able to be reached if I had something for him. I was to talk to his secretary first."

Deacon looked to us. "Warren had talked to the secretary when he went to Docktor's office to arrest him. She said she didn't know where he was. I may need to talk to her again."

"The secretary is a man," Joel said.

"What? I just thought it was a woman. I guess that's conditioning that makes me think that way and Warren never mentioned it. Okay, I'll talk to him. I'll have to talk to the D.A. to get you protective custody through their office. I can't imagine what Docktor would have against you since you were just passing info to him. Now, who could have told him that we talked to you?"

"Anyone who was helping in the church while we were decorating. Yvonne was in the church about the time you left after talking to me. She may have known."

"Well, I'm not going to ask her right now. Let's get you out of here." Deacon took Joel out to his car.

Trapper and I stood in the church looking around at the decorations they had put up. There were four men at the coffee table drinking. They must have been helpers. Angelo's men had gone back by Harold's office and were standing at the door.

"I hope Deacon gets something on her soon. I don't think she's good for Harold," I said.

"Ya think?" Trapper said with a grin.

People were starting to file into the building. I assumed they were there for Harold's service, since it was Sunday.

"Does he have late services on Sunday?" I asked.

"I don't know how he runs this place. I've only come in contact with him the few times we helped him. I've never been here for his church services and I don't want to start."

We turned and saw Yvonne coming out of Harold's office carrying lit candles, and then she went to put them on a makeshift altar. Harold came out dressed in a preacher's robe and stood at the altar watching the people sit in the chairs. More were coming in and the group was getting bigger. Trapper and I went to the back wall by the entrance and stood watching.

After everyone was seated, Harold came forward and said, "Thank you for coming and may the Lord's blessing be with you." He smiled at the small throng of worshipers and looked at Yvonne standing at the front edge of the stage. He nodded and smiled. He turned back and said, "I have an announcement before we start the worship. I have decided to sell the buildings and properties I own here on Industrial, close the church and move out of state. This is for my betterment and I'm sorry to leave all of you. There are two other churches in town that have services for the homeless and indigent. Now, if we can sing 'Greater to our God.'"

I turned to Trapper and said, "She works fast. I wonder who she's recommending he sell to?"

"I'm sure it won't be Docktor or Westeen. We'll have to come back and find out. Let's get out of here before I break out singing."

We went back out to the car and found Deacon still in his car with Joel. We moved over to his vehicle and Trapper told Deacon what Harold had announced.

"I know Sunday's are bad for getting work done by forensics, I hope they can pull a facial recognition off the video. I just got a call from Warren, he said background on Yvonne is a bust. Nothing in criminal records, or in personal files. Other than a driver's license, she doesn't exist."

"She'd need a driver's license to get married, so what are you going to do now?" Trapper asked.

179

Santa Murders

"Light a fire under forensics. I really want to nail this bitch. Care to join me back at the precinct?"

We agreed and followed Deacon out. At the precinct, Deacon led us to the CSI portion of the building. He entered a room with tons of electronic devices and went to one man at a desk. The man was working on a computer that was running faces at lightning speed.

"Hey Wally, are you running that face from the video?" Deacon asked.

"Still at it. I managed to get one good image of the woman from the video. Full frontal face and sharp. Should be able to get something if she's in the system."

"I'll bet you she is. Background on her came up negative, so I'm guessing she's hiding something."

"I've already run through most of the databases, so it won't be long now." Just as he said that, the computer made a noise and a photo popped up on the screen. "Wow, that was timing." He leaned forward and said, "Name's Yvonne Gajewski. From New York originally, married a wealthy man who turned up dead, but she wasn't suspected. Too many witnesses saw him walk into a bus." I couldn't help it, I chuckled. Trapper stared at me. I shrugged.

"Turns out she's been married a number of times, five to be exact," Wally continued. "Each husband died mysteriously, nothing to tie back to her though. The woman is good." The tech smiled. "Then she was going to be arrested in San Francisco, 2008, for scamming a man she married and tried to unsuccessfully murder. The husband suspected her and called the police. She fled the warrant and is on the run."

"I don't think Yvonne was counting on Harold having friends in the police to dig this deep," Deacon said.

"Are you going to arrest her now?" I asked.

"Wally, give me the info on the detective in charge of her last investigation. I think I'll call him to be sure."

The tech handed Deacon a piece of paper and we left the room. Back in Deacon's office, he got on the phone and called San Francisco police.

He finally tracked down the cop who handled the case of the missing bride. "I've got her here. Have you met her?"

The detective's voice came out of the speaker of the phone as we listened. "I talked to her a couple times when the husband suspected she tried to poison him. When we found out she did, we went to get her, she was gone. Hold onto that bitch. We have been looking into the prior cases involving the deaths of her previous husbands. She blew it by doing so many."

"How long would it take you to get out here? You deserve to arrest her," Deacon said.

"Well, thank you sir. I appreciate that. I'll grab a few men and we can be out there in a couple hours if we take the county jet. May as well use it."

"I'll give you the number of my sergeant and he can meet you at the airport."

"You've made my year, Lieutenant. Thanks."

"Call me Deacon, and we'll see you soon."

*

Chapter 27

Deacon hung up and smiled. "Well, it will be over soon. We'll be rid of her."

"I'm not trusting her. She's moving too fast. Firing Joel, getting Harold to sell his empire. Don't you think we should go watch her before she performs the matrimonial sacrifice of the praying mantis on Harold?" I said.

Deacon gave me a strange look.

"Praying mantises kill and eat their mates after they do the deed," I replied.

"I don't think we have to worry about Harold mating with her," Trapper said. "But I do worry about him ending up dead. I agree, we should watch her."

"Okay, I'll let Warren know where we'll be and have him bring the troops to the church." He went out to the squad room.

"We're working hard on this and we aren't getting paid for it," I said to Trapper.

"I'll hit Harold up with a bill when he sees the light of what she is all about. He can afford it."

"He'll be devastated when he finds out he's being used. I'd feel bad taking his money. But I'll only feel bad for a moment, since I can still picture all that money he hid in his attic. Have the police given back the money yet? I'd hate to see her get her hands on all that cash," I asked.

"Ask Deacon when he comes back."

On that cue, Deacon re-entered. I asked him about the money.

"We still have it locked up. Harold hasn't mentioned it and we are concerned that his life would be in jeopardy if he hid it back in the church. I told him he can get it Monday when the banks are open and that I'll send the money and a couple officers with him to deposit it."

"After we nab his wife, he may not want to go to the bank. I hope he doesn't get expensive lawyers to get her off the murder attempt," I said.

"Knowing him, he may try. We'll have to tie him down. Let's get out of here and go watch the flock."

Deacon called to Warren and said that we were leaving. Warren said he'd bring the men to the church.

We went to our cars and drove over to Harold's. At the church we could see all the people leaving the building. "Service must be over," I said as we approached the entrance. As we got there, Angelo's men were coming out too.

"Where are you two going?" I asked them.

One of the men said, "I'd rather incur Angelo's wrath than put up with that psycho bitch another day. I'm sorry, but with her, he doesn't need us. She fired us." They went off.

"This is getting worse. Let's go in," I said. We got to the door and it was locked. "What the hell." I rattled the door and then banged on it. I could see a light on in Harold's office through the small window beside the door, but no one was in the big room. The church was empty.

Deacon stood next to me looking in. "This isn't right. With all the attempts on Harold, I'm going to claim probable cause." He hefted his leg and took the door out with one kick. The noise brought Harold out of the office and he was surprised to see us.

"What are you doing? Why are you here?" he said as we came up.

185

"You tell me. What is going on here? You sent away your bodyguards, they were here to protect you."

"I never sent those men away. Are they gone?" Harold asked.

"Harold, you didn't notice that Yvonne is changing things around here? She's getting rid of everyone who hangs around the building, including your guards, as if she wants you isolated," Trapper said to the man.

"Will, why would she want to do that? She knew I needed to be protected."

We heard a noise from the back and saw Yvonne, accompanied by two men, coming out of the office. I was looking at the men, one was a shifty-looking, lower class person dressed in sloppy clothes. The other man looked more like a fancy lawyer—expensively dressed with the bearing of someone who knew what he wanted. I did notice that he was completely bald. Yvonne took them to a hallway on the side and they disappeared.

"Who's that and where are they going?" Deacon asked.

Harold turned to see them leaving. "I guess Yvonne is taking them out to the back door. They like their privacy."

"Who are they?"

"They're investors that Yvonne knew. I'm planning on selling the property and they made a generous offer."

"Why now, Harold?" Trapper asked. "This property has been in your family for a lot of years. You said you hated to sell your father's legacy."

"After all this trouble, I'm tired of it. Besides, Yvonne made me see that I'm better off selling it."

"Harold, have you asked yourself why this woman is in your life all of a sudden?" Trapper inquired.

"It was fate. We were destined to meet," he said.

"Okay, what about Lila? You loved her, too. Is she out of your life now that Yvonne is in it?"

Harold had to stop and think about that. "Lila will still be in my life, not like Yvonne is, but I still have feelings for Lila."

"Does Yvonne know about your fling with Lila?" Trapper asked.

"Who's Lila?" Yvonne asked, coming from the back of the building. She had to be listening. She came up to us, her eyebrows raised.

"My dear, she is a woman who I was involved with before you, but she's out of my life," Harold said, trying to spin the situation.

"Are you talking about Lila Westeen? Does her husband know about the two of you?"

Deacon spoke up, "He does know all about it and he's fine. Since he's off with his new love. Tell me Yvonne, where are you from?"

"What business is it of yours?" she asked.

Deacon held out his badge and said, "I have the power to ask questions when I feel there is a crime being committed."

"What crime, we've committed no crime," she said.

"Not yet, but we are going to be watching you. Besides, we have a surprise for you soon."

Deacon's phone buzzed and he answered. He turned his head away from us so he wouldn't be heard. I was standing next to him and could hear him say, "Warren, where are you?" He paused a moment before saying, "Good, go around the back of the building and make sure no one leaves. Send them in the front."

He turned and smiled. "Yvonne, do you remember San Francisco?"

Her eyes grew wide and she stuttered, "What do you mean?"

The front door opened and in came the detective from San Francisco. He grinned when he saw Yvonne. She wasn't grinning back. She turned to run to the back, the cops from Frisco ran after her and we followed. She got to the back hallway when she saw Warren was standing at the door. She turned down another hall and went through the buildings outer shell, where the factory had once stood and was now just walls. We were in pursuit as she moved quickly. Faster than we imagined she could run.

She found a flight of stairs and ran up them. We followed and figured we had her cornered. But when we got to the attic from this side, she was holding a Tiki torch she found and had lit the thing with a lighter she had.

"Stay away, or I'll set fire to this place," she yelled while backing up, holding on to the pole of the torch out front to keep us back. Deacon let the Frisco detective move forward.

"Yvonne, do you think you'll get out of this? I've got men below who will take you down."

She continued to back up and stepped on a piece of piping. It rolled under her foot. She went down as the Tiki torch set fire to a rack of old dry clothes. It went up fast and the flames were intense. Everyone backed away as we watched Yvonne try to stand by grabbing the rack to pull herself up, but the rack of clothes fell over on top of her.

I was watching and knew she couldn't have survived that.

*

Chapter 28

Everyone was trying to quell the flames by beating on them with whatever they could find. Someone ran down and grabbed a fire extinguisher and came back up to hit the fire. I had already called the fire department as the men worked to keep the fire from spreading. But the attic was old and full of flammable items that kept the fire moving. There was not much we could do. Two of the cops from Frisco managed to get the clothes rack off Yvonne and pulled her away. She was badly burned, probably dead already. I couldn't tell.

We all went back downstairs and could hear the sirens of the fire company coming quickly. Everyone was moving outside as the ladder truck pulled up and extended to hit the roof of the building with its hoses. The fire hadn't broken through the roof yet, but the water would wash down once a hole opened.

I moved back to the curb to watch and see if they could stop the fire before the entire building was engulfed. A building that old, eighty years at least, was prime for tinder.

The EMS unit had been dispatched along with the fire trucks, and the med techs were covering Yvonne's body. They pronounced her dead, she probably sustained too much injury coupled with smoke inhalation. Joe Lang would give the final pronouncement after he determined the cause of death. Harold was having fits over the body. Trapper was trying to subdue him and pulled him away from her.

I went to them and looked to the detective from Frisco. He came over. "Harold, listen to me," Trapper was yelling at Harold over all the noise from the hoses and fire. "This man is Detective Harry Morton, he's from San Francisco and he was here to arrest Yvonne for murder and fraud. She has a record and a warrant out for attempted murder and is suspected in other deaths of men she married. Her name wasn't Yvonne Wahl, it was Yvonne Gajewski, she was from New York."

Harold was staring in disbelief, then looked to Detective Morton. "Are you sure it was her?" he sobbed.

"One hundred percent sure. That's why she ran, she recognized me from when I questioned her when she tried to murder her fifth husband. I'm sorry, but it was her. She's a criminal, or was," he said, looking to the EMTs loading her in the unit. "If she hadn't been killed, we were going to take her back to Frisco."

Harold slumped a little and turned to see the building in flames. I could see the fire was mostly contained to the attic, maybe the quick actions of the firemen would spare the first floor. I thought about all the money that had been hidden up there and was glad it was safe in jail.

About an hour later, the firemen were examining the building. They had saved the main floor, most of the damage was in the attic. Luckily, the cops had worked prior to the firemen arriving to keep the fire from spreading too far. The building was originally a box factory, so it helped that provisions were in place to prevent fire from spreading in case of an emergency.

We were sitting in the chairs for Harold's congregation, watching the fire chief inspect the building. He pronounced it safe and no hot spots were found with their testing equipment. Deacon thanked them as they packed up everything to go back.

Harold looked so miserable. He lost a wife and most of his building and he was now alone, even his helpers were gone. I called Angelo and asked him to retrieve the bodyguards after explaining what happened with the wife. I also called Joel and told him to come back. He sounded happy and said he would be back.

Deacon sat next to Harold. "I know everything is hitting you fast, but I need to know, who were the men in your office when we got here?"

Harold had bloodshot eyes that he turned to Deacon. "They were investors from LA who wanted to build a hotel and casino on this property."

"What were their names?"

"Uh, the bald man was Otto Bruner and I don't remember his associate's name, it was difficult to pronounce. Something in German."

"Otto Brunner, from LA." Deacon looked to Warren and nodded. Warren pulled his magic tablet and punched in the name.

"Did you sell to them, Harold?"

"I was getting ready to do that when you came busting through the door."

"Maybe a good thing we did," Deacon said. He looked to Warren and waited for something.

"Brunner is clean, but he's being watched by the FBI for possible criminal activities. Nothing definite, but a suspect."

"Harold, this place is lousy with smoke," Trapper said, "take some of your money and get a nice hotel suite and rest."

Harold smiled and said, "Maybe I'll buy a hotel and take the penthouse."

"Or you could buy a whole motel and set up your church again, complete with living spaces for you and the homeless." I wasn't giving up on the idea.

"You're talking about that motel for sale?" he said with a smile.

"I've talked to my wife and we started the ball rolling for investors to buy it, but if you'd like to invest, you could take care of the place and live there."

Harold looked around at the high-ceilinged room, now covered in smoke stains and water. It would take a lot to fix up. The smell would last a long while, and the water had loosened what smelled like mold.

"I guess I'll sell my properties and invest in your project, Jim. Thanks. Now I have to get away from all this mess and start a new life."

"Oh, and you can forget about the marriage to Yvonne. She falsified her name so the license and marriage would be void," Trapper said. That cheered Harold a little.

Morton told Deacon, "I'll take my men back to Frisco, too bad I don't have a trophy to go with us." He gathered his men and Warren took them back out to his car.

My cell phone buzzed and I went to the side to answer. Caller ID said it was Penny. Probably to remind me about her dinner party. "Hey, babe. How's the party setting up?"

"Good, are you coming or not?" she asked.

I explained about my afternoon at Harold's. She listened and then said, "Well, why don't you bring Harold, too. There is going to be enough food for everyone. Fred is already here, he's a wiz in the kitchen. This man is a miracle."

"I'll ask Harold, but you'll have to let Trapper come, too."

"Fine, we'll still have more women than men. Be here by seven," she said then hung up. The Queen had spoken.

I went back to the men and smiled at Trapper. "What are you grinning about?" he asked.

"Penny is going to set up Harold with a bevy of women. You're invited, too."

"Is this the dinner you mentioned earlier?"

"Yep, Fred is already there and we need to clean up before we eat. I think Harold can use my guesthouse to clean up. Why don't you and he go get some nice clothes from his living quarters that don't stink from smoke."

Trapper grinned and went to get Harold. He asked what was going on. Trapper just smiled and said, "You'll like it."

*

Chapter 29

The church was closed up, Joel offered to stay overnight to be sure all was well in the building and no one robbed it. Angelo's bodyguards showed up again and were pleased to not have to deal with the she-devil, as they called her. They didn't say this too loud so not to offend Harold. Trapper and I took Harold to my guesthouse and he got ready for the dinner party. Fred remembered Harold and it was good they knew each other. Penny welcomed Harold, saying she was sorry for all the problems he was having.

This was the first time we had such a party in the house. Fancy dinner, real plates and nice friendly guests. We had picnics in the back for our friends many times, but never for Penny's co-workers. She invited her producer Gordy, but he had prior obligations. Penny invited Deacon and Lynn just to have our friends there in case all the women gave Fred and Harold their attentions. Which they did.

Harold was telling the women his adventures of the last week, from the kidnapping to getting married. Then losing his wife in the fire. They all gave him sympathy and then he explained that she was a murderous woman who married and killed her husbands. I noticed he slipped in the fact that he was rich, that impressed the ladies. Fred just sat enjoying the storytelling.

We were all settled in and enjoying the buffet Penny and Fred had set up. The food was delicious and plenty. I knew I'd be well fed for a few days. We all sat in the family room eating and talking. I had Angelo's men in to eat and they sat behind me on folding chairs.

Deacon, Trapper and I sat talking about the day. Deacon said, "I'm going to try to get a bead on this Otto Bruner to see what his link is to all this. He had to know Yvonne for her to invite him to buy Harold's property. He must have a history with her."

One of Angelo's men cleared his throat and said, "Excuse me, but did you say Otto Bruner?"

We turned our attentions back to the men. Deacon said, "Yes, do you know him?"

"I work for a guy who hires out pros for…well, attitude adjustments." He smiled and continued. "This guy used to get called occasionally from Bruner when he needed someone to take care of someone. If you know what I mean."

"The guy you worked for, what was his name?"

"Art Fremlin, nasty piece of work. I was just a messenger for him to find these men he wanted to hire."

"So you know where all the hitmen are hidden in Vegas?" I asked.

He just grinned and continued, "This Bruner guy called the last time to hire a man to take care of a problem regarding one of the mob bosses. Guy named Collisi."

That got our attention. We turned around to face him now. "How long ago was this?"

"Week before last. I still work for Fremlin, but I'm loaned out to Angelo for now."

"Do you know where Bruner does his business?" Deacon asked.

"I don't know, but I'm sure Fremlin does. He knows where everyone is so he can collect his fees."

"Where is this Fremlin doing his business?" Deacon asked, now looking hopeful.

"He has a small office up east of Fremont Street. I can give you the address if you need his services."

Santa Murders

"I think you may need to put your resume in elsewhere," I said to him with a grin. I pointed to Deacon and said, "You know he's a police homicide detective, don't you?"

The man gave Deacon a look then we heard him say quietly, "Oops."

"What's your name?" Deacon asked.

"Mario," he replied meekly.

"Well, Mario, I won't tell where we got this information, if you agree to help us track down this Bruner."

He gave us a big toothy smile and said, "Most assuredly. Be my pleasure. I never liked Fremlin or Bruner. Besides, Angelo said if I ever needed a job, he could set me up."

I quietly leaned to Trapper, "I said Angelo probably was getting a family together." He agreed.

"Okay Mario, just enjoy the party. Tomorrow is Monday and we have a lot of planning to do."

Everyone just sat back and enjoyed themselves.

At the end of the night, Harold said he was going back to the church and the two men went with him. Harold thanked Penny and me for the lovely evening, then they departed. I hoped they would be safe back in the church. I noticed Deacon was talking on his cell phone and then finished. I went to him.

"What evil are you up to?" I asked.

"I just called to have surveillance put on the church, just in case. Two cars, one in front, one in back. That should keep them safe for the night. I called Weber earlier and explained everything to him. He's a happy little man, now that he knows we are bringing down a ring of hitmen in Vegas."

"They'll just import ones from LA," I said. He gave me a frown.

He and Lynn said goodbye to Penny and me. All of Penny's co-workers left, they had to work in the morning. Trapper said he'd give Fred a ride back to the office. So everyone was gone. It was quiet in the house. Willy came out of the bedroom, now that they all had gone. He jumped up on me sitting on the couch, Penny brought out a beer for me and one for her.

"Do you want to watch TV here or go into the bedroom and watch TV from the bed?"

I looked at her and said nothing. "Okay, it's bedtime," she said.

Santa Murders

~~*~~

Otto Bruner was fuming. "I'd like to know why and how Yvonne died? We couldn't see in the building to know what was going on. I want the names of the responsible parties. Then call Fremlin and arrange to have them taken out."

"You know that's not a good idea. Most of the people there were cops. You kill a cop, you can hang it up."

"Well, I want revenge for Yvonne. If we hadn't left the building we may have saved her. That was my error. It won't happen again. I don't know if Renford will sell the property now that she is gone. We need to adjust our plans."

"Maybe he's still interested. You should contact him tomorrow and see. If you can convince him and get the papers signed, it will be over. Then you'll have the property."

The bald man sat thinking. "This whole thing was a mess from the start. I wanted the property so badly, I wasn't thinking right. Westeen is off with his lover and his wife rots in jail. At least they are out of the running to buy the property. My plot to frame Lila Westeen for the killing of Collisi blew big chunks and framing her boy toy, Renford, wouldn't get me the property. Now I'll have to go negotiate with him. At least we started a dialog today on selling the property. We need to start early, before he gets away."

*

Chapter 30

Morning came early with a phone call from Deacon. I was hoping that no one got murdered. I was wrong.

"Jim, we got Docktor. He's on a slab in the morgue," Deacon said as I tried to wake up. My clock on the stand said 7:15. I wasn't going to yell at him for waking me up earlier than my required time frame. When I heard Deacon say Docktor was dead, I got up.

"Okay, talk to me," I said as I stood, trying to get my body straight. The muscles and bones groaned.

"One of our cars was patrolling the strip and saw a car in one of the alleys behind Harrah's off

Koval. They approached the car and saw a man at the wheel, he was dead. Identification said he was Docktor. We can wrap that man up. Now we need to find out who killed him. I may send Mario in to ask Fremlin if he hired a hitman."

"I hope Fremlin doesn't suspect anything and take Mario out," I said.

"I'm having Mario wired, so he'll be safe. If you want to join us, we're leaving in an hour."

"You don't give an inch as to who you wake up, do you? I'll be there."

"I'll be in the undercover van with electronics division. See ya." He hung up and I got ready.

Penny was just heading out the door and stopped to kiss me. She took Willy with her, knowing I was going to be out chasing criminals. "I'll be stopping at the office, so if you're not too busy, come by." She laughed and went out after kissing me again.

I was on my way to see Deacon. I enjoyed being on surveillance with them. I liked spying on people.

I arrived at the van in the parking lot and went in. Deacon was getting Mario ready for his big acting debut and wired up. After a few warnings and instructions to Mario, he went out to his car and we followed him up to Fremlin's office.

We watched through the video monitors mounted on the van and Deacon said, "I've got cars all around the building. I don't know if this Fremlin is ready to fight."

We listened as Mario went in the building. "Hey, Art, how's business?"

We heard the man say, "Not bad, it's a good week for murder," he laughed.

"Really, who was murdered while I was gone?" Mario asked.

There was a pause, then we heard Fremlin say, "I had Stephan hired to knock off some guy name Docktor. It was done this morning."

"Well, good for Stephan. Who hired him?"

"Why would you want to know that?" Fremlin asked.

"No reason, I just like to know what to expect."

There was a pause again, then Fremlin said, "Okay, Bruner hired him. Docktor was getting in the way of some deal he was trying to do. I don't ask details, I just send the men in to bump off these mooks."

Deacon said, "We got enough, let's move in and be sure to arrest Mario so he's not suspected by Fremlin. We can use his testimony later."

About twenty minutes later, the police had the men in custody. I thought it was a quick detail and watched as they loaded the men in the police transport van.

"That's done, now we need to nab Bruner and it will be over," Deacon said with glee.

"Fine, but who will buy Harold's property?" I asked.

"I called Westeen out in Lake Mead this morning and explained the situation to him. I may not like the man, but he's willing to buy the property. He said he's heading back into town to talk to Harold."

"I thought Westeen didn't have the money?" I asked.

"He said that he talked to some investors and they would help out."

"Whatever, as long as Harold doesn't get stiffed," I said.

We were back in the precinct and all the players were rounded up and in custody. Fremlin finally gave up the location of Brunner. Deacon was more than happy to go arrest Brunner.

Charges were being filed on Bruner and Fremlin. Deacon had Mario moved to another area of lock up before releasing him. Mario said Angelo would protect him and had a deal to work for him.

I would have to have a talk with Angelo about his activities. Should be interesting.

Deacon said he was having Harold brought in to take custody of his money. Harold showed up around 10 am and had the one bodyguard with him since Mario was busy. Deacon assigned a couple officers to go along as Harold chose a bank to work with. He went with Nevada State Bank.

Harold asked me to come along to help him with the transactions. I hated banks, but had experience with them, so I agreed. Two hours later, Harold had his money safely in an account.

"We need to talk about this motel thing, so when you have time, we'll talk," Harold said to me. I was glad he was still considering it.

His bodyguard went off with him as I drove to my office. I was done with Deacon and his arrests. I was sure Captain Weber was delighted with the arrests and Deacon could maintain his standing with the man.

I arrived and found Willy and Henry in the dog run. No one was in the back, so I went in the building. I walked up the hallway to my office, but stopped at Trapper's door. He wasn't in. I went to my office and sat waiting to see who would show up first. It was Penny.

She came in and plopped down on my lap. "So sweetie, how was your day?"

"Not bad, I stood around watching the police arrest everyone involved in the Santa murder," I replied.

"So who was the dastardly person to frame Santa?"

"Some guy named Bruner. He wanted Harold's property and hired a hitman to get things in motion. It didn't work out in his favor and he finally brought our femme fatale Yvonne in to woo Harold, but that went south for her and Harold has agreed to sell to Ben Westeen for a hefty price. Oh, and Harold is going to help finance the motel shelter."

"That's real good to hear. Now, what do you have to do with this case?"

"Nothing, it's closed. Everyone has been arrested and charged. Now it's up to the courts and lawyers to work out punishments. The evidence is all there. So it will be a slam-dunk trial. How did your co-workers enjoy the dinner party?"

"They were all intrigued by Harold and Fred both. I think Harold more, since he's rich. Hey, they are desperate women. I don't blame them, I was liking Harold myself."

"I'm rich too, you know, and you are worth more than I am. So you don't need anyone else."

She kissed my nose and said, "I guess I'll keep you."

*

Chapter 31

The trials went well, everyone was sentenced to prison. I enjoyed that Brunner was going to be incarcerated for a long time. Harold was pleased and worked out a deal with Westeen to sell the property to him. Harold was going to be a wealthy man. He and I were in talks with Penny, Fred and three other people from the local homeless shelters and soup kitchens about converting the motel into a decent place for the homeless. We added another group with the people who ran the domestic violence shelters and could put them in the motel also. We were going to try and take care of everyone.

I finally got some time in to go shopping for Penny's gift, I had a perfect idea for what she'd like. I took Fred with me, just to have company, and I thought he would get a kick out of where we were going. We spent the day shopping and had lunch at Angelo's. I told Fred not to mention to Penny that I brought him here. Angelo joined us at our table and we talked about hitmen and the local mob scene. I was trying to pin Angelo down as to whether he had his own little family growing. He didn't admit to anything. I let it go.

The firm was picking up and everyone was busy chasing bad guys and cheating spouses. Okay, cheating spouses were money. So, we tolerated them. The money was coming in and we were doing well. I gave Lacey and Tracey a raise and everyone else was on a percentage so they enjoyed the better income.

Vegas was going through winter now, but it was not like Michigan winters, thankfully. Here, the nights were cold but it warmed up during the day. Christmas was coming fast and it always amazed me to see people watering their lawns so close to the holidays. Penny and I called back to my family in

Michigan to see how they were doing and wished them a Merry Christmas. We told them we would be coming out soon.

Christmas Eve came and we were having all our friends over to the house to exchange gifts. I gave Penny a toaster oven and she said quietly, "I'm going to kill you." I laughed.

It was a good night and Penny was glowing. Finally, everyone left and I said I was going to bed.

"So, what did Santa bring me?" she asked.

"I don't know. He won't come if we don't go to bed."

"You'll find any excuse to get me in bed. I suppose I have to earn my gift."

I just smiled and headed to the bedroom.

Early the next morning, Willy was bouncing on me, I was sure Penny put him up to it. I got up and put on my robe and went out to the living room. Penny was sitting on the floor in front of the Christmas tree holding the box that held her present from me. She had a childlike expression. I sat on the foot stool and told her to open it.

She tore into it and when she opened the inner box, she squealed. She brought out a brand new silver

211

plated Smith and Wesson .38 Special. "That's real silver, not cheap nickel," I said.

"Are the bullets silver too?" she asked with a grin.

"Only if you run into werewolves."

She handed me a big box and I opened it. Inside was a complete collection of all the entire seasons of 'Magnum P.I.' and next to that was a complete collection of 'NCIS' on DVDs. I loved it.

"Can I go out and shoot someone?" she asked examining the gun.

"You'll do that soon enough, I'm sure. I'll take you to the range and you can test it."

"I'm feeling stirrings," she said with an evil grin.

I stood and headed back to the bedroom. "Leave the gun out here," I said.

~~*~~

Epilogue

Six months later… We were all dressed up and waiting outside of the newly renovated motel to christen the opening of the new shelter for the homeless. Penny had her show's camera crew there to record the event and we had invited numerous public officials and the newspapers. Camera crews from the local TV news were in attendance. All our friends and our firm's family were there. Fred had brought a few of his friends from the tunnels to be the first residents of the shelter.

I went to the podium at the gateway to the motel and tapped the microphone. "Hello everyone. Most of you know me, I'm Jim Richards and this is my wife, the infamous Penny Wickens." I motioned to her standing next to me. "I'd like to welcome everyone here today to open a dream I've had for a number of years. A shelter for the homeless, troubled and lost souls of Las Vegas. It's my honor to introduce the man who will head up the daily operations of the shelter, Harold Renford." There was a good amount of applause as Harold took the podium and thanked everyone. He talked for a short while about the mission of the shelter and then thanked everyone. He turned to me as I handed him the big scissors to cut the ribbon. He went forward, cut the ribbon to officially open it up. Penny and I watched everyone walk into the lot of the building as Penny turned to me. "We did good."

THE END

Enjoy a preview of
Wiseguy Murders by Bob Moats

Chapter 1

Buck and Mac were making another trip around the perimeter of the newly renovated two-story motel, now a shelter for the homeless along with survivors of domestic and sexual violence. Buck's guards were patrolling the grounds due to the occasional fights and minor violence that occurred by the disadvantaged homeless persons who felt others were against them. Most of these people came from the streets or out of the flood tunnels from below the city of Las Vegas and the huge motel converted to a shelter was now a place to get away from the harshness of living in hostile areas. But they still weren't trusting of others and guarded their meager belongings carefully.

When the shelter first opened, it was decided that Buck would have his security guards stationed around the building to help prevent any outbreaks of violence that may occur. The motel was set-up for the safety of the people who lived there, but a lot of the people weren't happy about having to share a room with others.

Reverend Harold Renford was the coordinator of the shelter and since he had many years of experience dealing with the homeless, he knew it was not going to be a totally friendly place. Those persons who were survivors of domestic and sexual violence were separated from the living quarters of the homeless. The DV shelter was administered by a local organization that provided help and shelter to abused spouses and children. They were short of rooms to house all the needy people in their own shelters, so our shelter was offered as an extra place to house the overflow.

Penny and I would visit frequently to see how things were going, since we had spent a good amount of our own money to buy the motel and renovate it. Harold was wealthy and he had been rescued by Trapper, Deacon and me from the clutches of people wanting to steal his money and valuable land property. After we solved the Santa murder case, I convinced Harold to invest in the motel. He was more than happy to help with his generous funding. He also lived on the premises, which helped to maintain his presence with the people. Many knew him from the old church he had before he sold the property to developers who wanted to build more casinos and hotels for the people who didn't have to worry about where their next meal was coming from.

The big community room in the shelter was converted into a makeshift church for Harold's Sunday worship, and used as a cafeteria to feed the vast number of people who took refuge there. A kitchen was built in the back of the room and served hot meals three times a day. Harold and I had talked to a number of community agencies and wealthy financiers about donating money, food and other necessities to help make the stay at the shelter as pleasant as possible. There were also on-site counselors and job placement personnel to get many of the people back on their feet and out of the shelter into better lives.

Lacey's husband, Mac, was running the security portion of my investigating firm now that Buck was a licensed investigator, and busy with his own cases. I suggested to Mac to get a number of the homeless men involved in a patrol of the property to help keep the peace. That would give them a sense of pride in helping with the daily operations of the shelter and earn a small wage to help them out.

Bob Moats

The newest member of my little family, Fred Jarvis, was a big help around the place. Fred had been a homeless person himself, before I helped get him out of the tunnels. He became a valuable part of my firm. He also knew a number of the homeless, many who looked up to him since he made it out of the tunnels—he gave them hope. Fred still had his work to do in our own building—cleaning, lawn care and guarding the building at night—but he would go over to the shelter to help when he could. We got him a car, so he had more freedom to move around.

Buck had time to kill this particular day, so he joined Mac in making the rounds to check on the guards. In one section of the building, they came to a half-opened door to one of the rooms. Mac decided to check and see if everything was all right. He pulled his huge flashlight and shined it into the room, since there were no lights on.

"Hello? Everything all right in there?" Mac called into the room. He glanced at a plaque on the front of the door which had the names written of the people who shared the room. At present, there were only two persons assigned to this room. Buck came up behind Mac and yelled in also. There was no reply. Mac went further into the room and reached to the wall switch, turning the room light on. The overhead light brightened up the room, now painted in bright colors to hopefully cheer up the residents.

Santa Murders

There was no one in the room. Mac approached the half-opened bathroom door, and pushed the door open wider. He paused, looked back to Buck and said, "I think we need the police." He moved back so Buck could look in. Buck saw the man hanging by the neck with a rope tied to the shower rod.

~~*~~

I was visiting Penny at her studio while she was interviewing a famous movie starlet, Lorna Jackson, about a film she had just wrapped up in Vegas. I didn't go to the studio very often, but today I had nothing better to do and I wanted to visit with my wife for once at her place of work. She always came by my office to bug me before having me take her out to get lunch.

Gordy, Penny's producer, came up behind me and I jumped when I saw him. "Sorry, I've learned to move very quietly around the studio while we tape the show," he said with a smile. "What brings you here today? No crimes, I hope." Gordy reached out to ruffle Willy's head as I held the tiny dog.

"No, just slumming. I thought I'd come in to watch Penny do her stuff," I replied.

"Besides looking at Lorna Jackson?"

"Well, she is a big star and not hard on the eyes," I said with a grin.

"Our ratings go up when she's on the show."

"How are the ratings doing? I know the survival of her show is in the ratings."

"Penny's safe, her ratings put her in the top ten of daytime programming. It will take a lot to bump her off," Gordy replied with his chest out. He was proud to have been with Penny from the start, moving with her from the little local cable show back in Michigan. He fought to get her back into a network spot after she quit the first show when she was upset by the way things were handled by management regarding her guests being killed.

"I hope she hangs in there. A happy Penny is a happy Penny," I said with a laugh.

The show ended and the audience was moving out of the studio. Gordy excused himself and went off to do his job. I slowly went back to Penny's dressing room and in to see the flurry of people getting her make-up off and dressed for the day. She saw me in the mirror and waved as I sat and placed Willy next to me. He yipped once seeing her. All the girls in the room laughed at his attempt to call to her.

Santa Murders

As I sat, my cell phone buzzed. I debated whether to answer, but I did since the caller ID said it was Buck. I was sure Penny could tell by my frown that there was a problem.

*

Continued in the book...

~~*~~

Jim Richards Family of Readers

Thanks to the following people who are now part of the Jim Richards Family of Readers. They have read a book or more and enjoyed them. They all volunteered to be included in the list. If you are a fan of the books, send me your full name and you will be included in future books. Send your name to murdernovels@bobmoats.com to be added here and on the website. (updated 03-26-14)

* Achim Feifel * Al Norris * Alex Wheatley * Alexandra Delporte-Wilkinson * Amy Tapia * Andrea Bryan * Anne Shepherd * Arianda Sugar * Arlene Markowski * Ashley Augustus * Audra Hall * Barbara Hughes * Barbara

Bob Moats

Sammons * Barbara Schuler * Barbara Zirger * Beth Donohue Plenskofski * Betsy Childress * Beth Gibson * Bill Sandy * Bill Tornquist * Billie-jo Collie * Boni J Rychener * Carl Bishopric * Carla Lewis * Carole Henderson * Carolyn Conroy * Carolyn Riddle-Linington * Cassy Bailey * Chad Hudson * Charlotte L Duran * Cheryl L. Everett * Cindy Ackley Nunn * Cindy Valstad * Connie Bancroft * Corinne Kay O'Daniel * Dana Robbins Chuchran * Dana Wichita * Danielle Monique * Darren Heald * Dave Travers * David Wilkinson * DeAnn Jannereth * Deanna Miller * Deb Breuker Balbo * Debbie Carter * Debbie White * Deborah Fartuch * Deborah Gauze * Deborah Sullivan * Dee King * Denise Freeman * Diana Carver * Dixie Beck * Donna Gould * Donna Thompson * Donny Minter * Doris Kight * Eddie Moore * Eric Walters * Felicia Annette Bradfield * Francine Menor * Gail Chesney * Georgiann Minster * George Conner * Greg Colucci * Hayley Rankin * Harold Garcia * Heidi Arnold * Irma Ranee Coy * Jacqueline Moss * Jan Kimball * Janice Schneider * Janice Spoor * Jennifer Redmond * Jessica Keown-Belous * Jim Beck * Jo Boguslaw * Jo Turner * Joanne Marie Turner * John Peiffer * John Wisbiski * Joseph Wauro * Joyce Stacy * Joyce Trifiletti * Judy Franklin * Judy Travers * Judy Padgett * Julie Heath * Junnahvee Benson * Karen Dahl * Karen Grams * Karen Higham * Karen Kaiser * Karen Meinburg Richwine * Karen Kirkman Parker * Karin Hawkins * Karin Vasvari * Kathleen Donohue Roesing * Kathleen Riddle-Wolfe * Kathy Hinds Moore * Kathy Jones * Kathy Mitchell * Katie Benzler * Kay Burns * Kelly Garcia * Ken Boggs * Keota Rodriguez * Kiera Mccarthy * Kim Estes * Kitty Stolle * Kristie Sciler * Kirsty Stanton * LaLonnie Scallen * Larry Morris * Leann Parr * Lenora Scales * Leslie Marie Jackson * Linda Forester * Linda Ingle Cox * Linda Kennerö *

Santa Murders

Linda Magill * Lisa Bower * Liz Gibson * Lorraine Wiman * Loretta Alexander * Lynda Bowles * Lynette Lawrance * LuAnn Louttit * Manny Rothman * Marcia Gibson DeWitt * Marie Calder * Marlene Bryan * MaryLouise Kramp * Mary Lynn Gross * Megan Atkins * Meghan Hyden * Melody Cannavan * Michael Carruthers * Michael Dinkens * Michael Vannoy * Michelle Burns-Mitchell * Michelle Pilcher * Micki Potter * Mike Moats * Mimi Baur * Myrna Hecht * Nadine Sutton * Natalie Quine * Neena Martin * O'Della Wilson * Pat Pollington * Pat Rohn * Patricia Jarmon * Patricia C Trezza * Patrick Barry * Paul Lawrance * Peggy Davis * Phyllis Bassett * Raylene Matheny * Rebecca Collins Besner * Renee Brumley * Reta Hanna * Reta Moats * Roberta Navarro-Harder * Sally Berneathy * Sally Hubler * Sarah Santos * Satka Nikc * Sharon E. Edwards * Sharon Mangini * Sharon McMillon * Sheena Rawl * Sherry Amstutz * Shirley Alvarez * Shirley Davies * Shirley Williams * Stacie Rowe * Stephanie Conner * Steve Cullen * Susan Haughton * Susan Hesse Adams * Susan Salomon * Suzan K Chase * Taisha Cullum * Tamara Moore * Tammy Castleberry * Tammy Lynn Wood * Ted Murphy * Terri Atkins * Terri Creech * Terry Raab * Tonia Rachael Riggs-Williams * Travis Fleury-Lopez * Twyla Gawlas * Val Brooks * Walt Munsel * Yvonne Isakson *

Thank you to all these wonderful people.

www.ingramcontent.com/pod-product-compliance
Lightning Source LLC
Chambersburg PA
CBHW070816120626
46556CB00002B/532